SOLILOQUIES OF MY SOUL

Naida, dear,   11-6-16

May you always hear the loving
whispers of the angels and feel Gods
arms holding you in His comfort.
I am so grateful that He blessed me
with your presence in my life.

My love,
Marie

SOLILOQUIES OF MY SOUL

Poetry, Writings, Songs

Marie E. McFadden

Ravelings of time fed the day with colored threads
of thought.

Library of Congress Control Number: 2016915912
ISBN: Hardcover   978-1-5245-4559-8
                 Softcover   978-1-5245-4558-1
                 eBook   978-1-5245-4557-4

Print information available on the last page.

Rev. date: 09/24/2016

To order additional copies of this book, contact:
Xlibris
1-888-795-4274
www.Xlibris.com
Orders@Xlibris.com
746139

TABLE OF CONTENTS

WRITINGS

SONGS

Acknowledgment

I am forever grateful to God, my children, my extended family, and friends who have allowed me space in their lives. Much appreciation is sent to my sister for inspiring me to continue on when I felt helpless.

A special thank you to Mykah Charette, my granddaughter, for the time spent in typing and trying to decipher poems scribbled on scraps of yellowed paper that had been saved for many years. Her proficiency of English was a pleasant surprise.

To all of you walking this road of life, sharing your gifts of care and knowledge, giving your love of fellowship to those in need, I pray for you to receive eternal blessings.

Tammy Sund, my first grandchild, who has an extremely busy life, contributed hours of her time on the computer. She has always been a champion for Grandma. I do so appreciate her.

Silent Prayer

Oh, great and wonderful God,
Whose breath can ripple the ocean.
Whose hand can move a mountain.
He who can give sound to deafness.
Sight to those who never see.
Grant us this one small favor.
Thy will be done, Amen.

Marie E. McFadden

Dedication

To my grandchildren, for you are the joy and radiant colors of my ending sunset. I pray you can find words of faith, hope, understanding, and love within its pages. I am so proud of each and every one of you. Thank you, for the added blessings in the joy shared with my great-grandchildren and great-great-grandchildren.

Seth Lawton, Gabriel Shattuck, Tammy Sund, Tanya Nolan, Toni Cluphf, David Wyatt, Taaffe Wyatt, Shawn Ziemba, Benjamin Hanson, Megan Judy, Tiffany Bowman, Timika Harris, Lena Sanford, Angelia Smith, Natasha Pineda, Marco Flores, Joseph Vowels, Joshua Charette, Mykah Charette

With all my love,

G. Marie

Do not be afraid, little flock, for it is your
Father's good pleasure to give you the kingdom.
—Luke 12:32

Introduction

At night when the house was asleep, I'd sit on the bare wood floor by this upstairs window, and watch the moon turn the land into silver.

Merriam-Webster Collegiate Dictionary's definition of *soliloquies* is a dramatic monologue that represents unspoken reflections by a character. Yes, I have definitely been described as such a character. The crazy lady, sweet old lady, tough old broad, and the tomboy that Dad called Pete.

Eighty-six acres nestled in the arm of the Sol Duc River provided me mossy paths, deer trails, meadows, forests, and riverbank to wander and to ponder. Deep in the forest, I could hide fear and find some release from the emotional abyss. My roaming was never alone, for I requested God's presence.

My mind finally found its resting place in a twelve-step program to which the past thirty-seven years, leaves me forever grateful.

I hope my poetry, writings, and songs reflect the joy, tears, despair, and laughter of life that I shared with my family. "The good, the bad, and the ugly," as Clint Eastwood would say.

I pray if you relate to some of my writings, you will reach out for help and understanding. Life can be so full of hope and promise.

The Seasons

Tiny, purple, violets,
Daffodils, flocks of geese,
Fields of lupine
Plump pink apple blossoms, lilacs,
And sparkling droplets of sweet rain.
'Tis spring.

Morning's dew, steaming from warm brown earth,
Wild berries, singing birds,
Mason jars,
The old swimming hole,—
Freedom.
'Tis summer.

Red, gold, crimson,
Maple leaves, apple cider,
Fat pumpkins, frost,
Rashes of venison.
'Tis autumn.

Snow like angels talc,
Bacon rind hanging high in rafter,
Tiny footprints, pine boughs,
Trees like black lace filigree,
'Neath silver moon,
Christmas lights.
'Tis winter.

God enwraps the weary soul in beauty.
'Tis all remembered.

The Farm

Peeling carrots and taters on the old kitchen stool,
Fresh warm cow's milk set in water to cool.
Canning beans and corn, swiss chard and peas,
Putting apples in bins before the first freeze; This I'll remember forever.

The heel first cut from a fresh loaf of bread,
The funerals we gave when a bird was found dead.
The blossoms in spring covering all of the trees,
A run through lupines that grew up to our knees;
This I'll remember forever.

Running barefoot all day through stickers and grass,
Catching huge bumblebees in jars made of glass.
The first flock of geese flying south in the fall,
The baby calves cry and the old mother cow's bawl;
This I'll remember forever.

The old woodshed with wood stacked high,
The snowy white clouds or the blue summer's sky.
The jam to be made, fruit canned for winter,
Sliding over a log, the feel of a splinter;
This I'll remember forever.

The river raging, filled with fallen logs,
A playhouse in a stump, picking up apples for the hogs.
Chili made on washday, clothes off the line so clean,
Baths in a big old washtub, new baby calves to wean;
This I'll remember forever.

Laying in a haystack feeling the hot sun all over,
Picking ferns for throwing spears, sucking honey out of clover.
Sleeping in the hay all night in a great big barn,
A whole lifetime of memories, just made on our farm;
This I'll remember forever.

By the River

Here I sit by the river and dream,
Seeking the future, how far it seems.
Here dreams have been broken,
Thought of words never spoken.
Here by the river
And woods that are stilled,
Maybe someday here
Dreams will be fulfilled.

His Tears

I think of the rain as God's falling tears,
One's shed for mankind through sin laden years.
Each droplet creating mountains of green,
Rivers and oceans and beauty unseen,
By an uncaring world who would rather do evil,
And who worships material doings created by the devil.
The sorrow is heavy as drops wash my face,
How sad He must be when He looks at this race.
But there must be a few whose hearts fill with love,
For smiling He sends us warm rays from above.

The Rebellious Cry

Very gently, youth blew dust from the cover, then flicked the moldy page.
Studying the list of contents, he reflected upon a different age.
Hearing all of his life about the good old days, never would he understand
Why they were called good by people seemingly content,
When strife was ravaging the land.
He'd seen poverty and bigotry, heard the despair of the old.
Watched the young die in war, for reasons untold.
He'd choked on the smog, walked in the waste.
Saw the water polluted, unfit to taste.
Great men had written of this, hundreds of years before.
Following generations read, probed, discussed, but, did no more.
Youth studied the words,
From Lincoln on slavery, freedom and right;
About American Indians poverty and plight.
To ecology, preservation, war, and liberation, morals and dress,
Freedom of press, racism, draft, dope, and graft,
To the Kennedy's and king and all in between with a new song to sing.
He'd studied the words until his vision blurred,
And he knew in his heart that youth must be heard.
Apathy and stagnation were devouring a great nation.
He must show his strength, make wrongs into right.
In a world filled with darkness, cast a new light.
Carefully placing the old book on the shelf,
He straightened his shoulders preparing himself.
Age never before had heard such a cry,
As when youth walked in with head held high.

Revelation of a Summer's Day

It laid insignificantly amongst billions of its kind,
Bringing forth its true importance, readily to my mind.

Together with its counterparts, it formed a peaceful summer beach.
I weighed it testily in my hand, then threw it far beyond one's reach.

It landed amongst an alder row, where the brush was thick and dank.
Wherewith it then became a part of the river's bank.

I sought its whereabouts and threw it far over my head,
It slowly settled down to become a part of the flowing river bed.

Could I upon this earth move even a pebble so small
From one form or place to another, where it would not fit into God's
plan for all?

Each thing, each one, has its own space in time,
Truly the only thing I can ever really change, is this attitude of mine.

Oh, Maple Tree

Gaunt and knurled giant,
Arthritic limbs bent to earth,
Your covering loosened upon the ground.
Like an old man sitting by his hearth,
A patchwork quilt about his feet.

Awaiting spring's redressing
With visions of youthful adornment,
Forever stalwart you'll stand,
As naked as Adam in the beginning,
Through winter's destructiveness.

Old? What Is Old?

Old? What is old?
When my heart still likes to sing,
When laughter fills my breast,
And the barb of life has lost its sting.

Old? What is old?
I still work and love and play,
I share my faith with others,
I hold pity, loneliness, death at bay.

Would you have me close my door
On youth, on life, on dreams?
Would you have me shrivel inside
As well as out, or put away my self-esteem?
Would you have me sit with nothing
But only breath to show I live?

Old? What is old?
I have yet so much to give.

Cornucopia

Brilliant esplees of summer's hand,
Line my pantry's shelf.
Taunting winter's hungry grasp,
With plenty's store of wealth.

When cold embraces the windowpanes,
And north wind stalks his prey.
We'll remember summers beautiful days,
How quickly they passed away.

Forgotten will be the toil and time,
And prayers for a prosperous yield.
The table will be laden with a feast of jewels,
Like a gift from the masters field.

A Smile Shared

If you meet someone who hasn't a smile,
Please, give him one of yours.
Down through the years
We have an abundance of tears,
So if you meet someone who hasn't a smile,
Please, give him one of yours.

The brightest ray of sunshine on a cloudy day,
Can be a smile shared with others,
As they pass life's troubled way.
Passing down the ordinary street,
I've met people deep in thought.
I've witnessed friends in tragedy,
Known the battles they have fought.

A smile gives so much comfort,
There's so many who are in need
Of warmth and uplifting.
Please, hear the prayer I plead.
If you meet someone who hasn't a smile,
Please, give him one of yours.

I was prompted to write this poem,
In a moment of deep despair.
When a male nurse opened my door,
And a smile he had to share.
He didn't know how much I needed
Help at just that time.
But because he left that smile,
It became a smile of mine.

The Devil at Play

The devil rode on horseback,
Through my mind today.
Snatching at every precious moment,
Stirring up emotions to make me go astray.
He poked fun at love and sneered at happiness,
Openly laughed at my serenity.
Tried to invoke restlessness,
He thought he was an entrepreneur
When it came to salesmanship,
Deliberately set about to ruin relationships.
He used his expertise so elegantly,
To emphasize hate and fears,
And was extremely delighted,
When martyrdom brought on my tears.
But I was not lost nor disheartened,
My emotions were not easily swayed,
Though he gave his most experienced shot,
I was aware of the devilish games that he played.
Oh, well, he tried and lost I'd say,
For I try to walk with the grace of God today.

Quiet Observations

How very empty is an expanse of blue,
Unless you add a summer's sky, a drifting cloud or two.

Say to yourself, "Bubbling brook or rivers wide."
Now, envision their meeting with the oceans flowing tide.

See a distant star shining in the night,
Add a few moonbeams or a jet in silver flight.

Hear the wind whisper through the spruce and pine,
Then, listen for the hooting of the night owl,
Feel the tingle down your spine.

Watch a dandelion float gently on a breeze.
Do you see a meadow filled with flowers?
Do you hear the humming of the bees?

Enthralled by the beauty around us,
So much more can be heard and seen.
If we can see with an inner eye,
To all the happenings in between.

The Promise

From fancy resorts where men took their ease,
Over distant lands to the farthest seas.
From the Mojave desert to the West Indies,
Where ere before mankind had tread.
On deep jungle trails where ever they led,
To battlefields where blood was shed.
High atop majestic mountains peak,
Beside long river or some small creek,
Of valley floor and meadow I speak,
Walked this man I ne'er saw before.
Bending to pick and add to his store,
Bright shiny objects which made me implore.
"What is it you see? Tell me, please.
Why do you gather so many of these?
I see you searching through grass and trees."

He showed me the droplets in hand outspread,
Saying the great book in heaven was ready to be read.
All are being called the living and the dead.
No stone left unturned until the job is done.
Each single tear will be counted,
One by one.

Summer's Blessing

Mother Nature's breath turns chill,
Creating fog that enwraps the morn.
Fall freshly paints the lowland bush,
The spider crochets a web that's torn.

Ole Sol persistently tries to peek
At gardens plenty, being stored away.
Inhaling air that's heady cider sweet,
Jack Frost waits to ice the last fall day.

North wind prepares to expand his lungs,
He practices his howl and wail.
Patiently like a dedicated chemist,
Mixes the rain, the snow, the gale.

Ole Sol can hide his face, Jack Frost can paint.
The North wind can blow his very best.
The larder is full, the fireside warm.
God created summer, we were truly blest.

The Green Shades

A long time ago on a starless night,
We sat by the radio, our hearts twinged in fright.
The enemy it said, had declared war on our land.
Every able bodied man, must go make his stand,
For freedom and liberty, for justice, and right,
We looked up to Dad, and pondered our plight.
Would he have to go and leave us alone?
Would we lose our family, our country, and home?
Dad said he was sure he wouldn't be taken.
We were tucked into bed, our world was shaken.

The army moved in and built forts outside of town.
Along the road pill-boxes peeped above ground.
I remember the green shades that were hung with care,
For no light must be seen from planes in the air.
When a trip to the outhouse was made to and back,
Our old farmhouse looked eerie and black.
It was a long time ago on a starless night,
But I can still see the green shades, holding in the light.

May my children never know of green shades hung with care,
Only peace and goodwill that we all may share.

A Welcome to Spring

Freshly scented, yellow cups
Upon petaled saucers set;
Making winters wildest rage,
Easy to forget.

Bowing heads to showers of spring,
Nodding gently in a breeze,
Like nuggets of purest gold,
Cast beneath the trees.

Oh, beautiful daffodil,
Your welcome is sublime.
When we see your smiling face,
We know spring arrived on time.

Graveyard of Driftwood

Along the ocean side it lies,
Betwixt grey sand and summer skies.
Bleached remnant of sea and storm,
Now, dignified tree transformed.
A Spanish galleon beached forever,
Giant locomotive with brake and lever.
A child filled with imagery and dreams,
Revives its purpose and useful means.
An artist with brush and oil,
Paints its beauty with loving toil.
Its warmth is felt at fireside,
The flames burn strong with snapping pride.

Once it seemed its life was o'er,
Resigned to lay forever more.
As nothing, until its return to dust,
But by some miracle of thought, it became
A galleon coated with rust,
A painted picture with loving grace,
Or warmth and beauty in a fireplace.

Nature teaches wisely that we may learn,
When youth is lost we take our turn,
Like driftwood lying by the ocean side,
To await a need, a purpose,
In life's changing tide.

MARIE E. McFADDEN

Father Time

I remember the waiting in quiet anticipation,
Sweet chimes fulfilling awaited expectation.
Clear crystal notes that gently ruffled the air,
No sound of the day could ever quite compare.
Such magnificent music always came with surprise,
You felt betrayal when you lifted your eyes.
The old clock, I thought, very plain and forlorn,
Sitting high on its shelf; all scratched and worn.
Sadness always touched this child heart of mine,
When with accurate deliberation it began to chime.
I felt time slipping stealthily into the past,
Wishing I could catch it in my hand and hold it fast.
Death took grandfather silently to his breast,
And the ugly old clock came to our house to rest.
Mother decided one day to improve on its grace,
Under layers of old paint we found a new face.
Hand carved scrollwork and old father time,
With wise old owls in his beard entwined.
Decrepit old clock, who could have ever guessed,
The hidden beauty you carried, with each hour you blessed.
I've learned a lesson from grandfather's clock of old,
Beneath layers of age, there is beauty untold.

A Choice

I had toiled late to the midnight hour,
Then came to work at morn.
A fellow worker expressed concern,
"Now aren't you tired, weary, and worn?"
For just a moment in contemplation.
I thought about my body and my mind,
Then answered with a friendly smile,
"No dear, I'm feeling mighty fine."
You see, God gives me strength,
For the job to be done.
Gives ways to ease my body,
Through the last miles run.
With his support I've got a definite choice,
I won't let my mind dictate the blues.
It's up to me to be happy or sad,
And happy is what I choose.

Throes of Temptation

Look now, oh temptation,
Through iron bars of will.
Girded by faith and wisdom,
This hour is restful still.

Monstrous and demon-wise,
Twisting all feeling and thought.
Hirudinoid and devouring,
'Tis horrendous battle I've fought.

If I can but hold this day,
Cementing it to tomorrow.
With hope and peace of mind,
I'll have won the battle of temptation,
Leaving my fears behind.

Evening Tide Fog

When sun's warm hand
Is lifted from green meadow land,
A crisp white moon smiles over mountains blue,
Bringing dampness to settle in evening's dew.

Quietness enfolds the farm land still,
Birds of the air have chirped their last trill.
Creeping silently along the valley floor,
Hiding all from the sight of man,
Comes the evening tide fog,
Soft wisps of white like sifting sand.

There in the shadows,
Where the cattle low.
The scene is cast in an eerie glow,
Evening tide fog gives peace to the land,
And you can feel the touch of the master's hand.

Blame

Oh, whining remorseful soul,
Don't you realize
It wasn't your God
Who put tears in your eyes?
You tread down life's pathway,
Placing the blame,
Hunting for someone's shoulder,
To carry your shame.
Unhappiness and heartache,
Were made by your hand,
In the tar pit of sin,
You made your grand stand.
Well, it's no fault of His,
You're covered with mire,
He said to evade evil,
To cast your foot higher.
No, you wouldn't listen,
Satan became friend,
So why not blame him
For the trouble you're in?
If you ask God's help,
He'll not turn away.
Quit blaming and sinning,
Remember how to pray.
A long forgotten peace,
Will quiet your soul.
Once again to be cleansed,
Blessed, and whole.

Marie E. McFadden

Tree

Is there such a friend as have I
Sturdy tree stretching it's boughs to the sky.

Tell it words and it keeps your secret,
Like God keeps prayer,
In depths,
Never again to be spoken.

Many secrets does it know,
For centuries known,
The stories of the young and the old,
Still silence it keeps.

The Lighthouse

Apprising beacon,
Inquisitively poking your eerie eye.
Through dusks gray curtain,
Probing misty fog,
Or challenging distant star.
Dawn witnesses your architectural grotesqueness,
While sea birds rest upon your collar;
Yet ships of night verify your worth.

Westport

Oh, bay of blue.
With your trails of wispy white,
Capped by a cloudless sky,
And gulls in languid flight.
Embraced within the arms of land,
Protecting your ruffled skirt of sand.
Ever lifting your voice to heaven's door,
With gentle flow or mighty roar.

An Impression

I've always been guilty of first impressions,
They've never led me to be wrong.
When we shook hands you left apart of you,
That to me will always belong.

Though we barely met and said hello,
Apart of you I'll always remember.
When we shook hands and contact made,
I knew you to be strong yet tender.

I felt your friendly interest,
Your Christian warmth, felt too.
I knew you had good teaching,
That you could be tried, found true.

During the service, I watched you,
Your head bent in prayer.
I sent a prayer to God myself,
Please be with him everywhere.
Please keep him safe from the
World and all its unrest.
Please let him know his road leads right,
To all that's good and blest.

So shake a hand and leave a friend,
Where ever you may roam.
Unbeknown to us, that friend maybe
The one that welcomes us,
To our heavenly home.

Iron Chains

I must be able to readily recognize,
The iron chains of life that bind.
The freedom of my heart, of my soul,
And of my mind.

If I've filled my heart with hate and greed,
Turned away from those with outstretched hand.
Then He shall also turn from me,
For love was His greatest command.

If I have gained knowledge,
Yet let wisdoms bell toll for naught.
Then my mind will never know,
Why the battle has been fought.

If my soul is bound to earth and dust,
And cannot roam the heavens free.
Then I have not served my God,
Nor received the blessings He promised me.

Each day I must oil the hinges,
That opens the door of my heart.
Keeping the wick well trimmed,
On the lamp of wisdom,
So my soul can easily depart,
To the safety that He promised,
From the iron chains of life that bind,
Gaining the freedom of my heart, of my soul,
And of my mind.

MARIE E. MCFADDEN

Women's Lib You Say

Women's lib you say,
I'd like to know who needs it.
Isn't it supposed to be
Freedom for women's rights?
For ones who want equality,
Or have destinies in sight,
My destiny was planned,
A homemaker I would be.
I wanted to be the best,
It must have been granted me.
Every day's a wash day,
With laundry to be done.
By piles on the basement floor,
A Chinese laundry I could run.
My cooking I've been told,
Is the best within the City.
I cook like for an army,
My grocery bill's a pity.
There's sewing and there's ironing,
I'm always far behind.
Cleaning windows, scrubbing floors,
And washing off the grime.
Oh, destiny, I thought, not blunder,
While seven kids pillage and plunder.
If this be the reward of destiny,
I'd rather be six feet under.
Well, equality I looked for,
And wished I hadn't found.
For all the little tasks I do,
Conveniently, father is not around.
I had to learn about wrenches,
And the hammer and the nail.
I was quick to replace washers,
So I wouldn't have to bail.
Thirty weight oil or change a tire,

Fix a fuel line or unchoke a choke.
I could only drive the family car,
If I could fix whatever broke.
Load that barge, tote that bale,
The rewards of equality,
I'll leave to the male.
Freedom of women's rights,
It's something I've always had.
To do anything I wanted,
If it didn't interfere with Dad.
Whatever you want to do,
Do it, if you want to, honey.
I really want you to express yourself,
If it doesn't cost me money.
Destiny I cannot shirk,
Though it's a lot of work.
Equality I have to take,
Even if my back will break.
Freedom really lost its' meaning, so, I might as well stop dreaming
Women's lib you say, I'd like to know who needs it!

Angel's Reflection

I have the ability within my soul,
To love more fiercely than you'd 'ere believe.
To love more tenderly and everlasting,
Twice as I'd ever expect to receive.
Could it be to love so greatly
Would not be right?
Perhaps, the angels would resent
Such love blinding
One's daily sight.

Your Will And Mine

Dear Lord, I'd like to thank you,
For such a perfect day,
For all my loving family,
And for friends you sent my way.
I'd like to thank you for tribulations, too,
That came about in this day's work.
Though patience and ability were tested,
My faithful duties I did not shirk.
This evening I may sit in gratitude,
Appreciating peace at twilight time,
Knowing that I've successfully accomplished,
Both your will and mine.

Tasty Bite

I'm not very good at rhyming or prose,
But I must tell this tale of a little boy's nose.
He wasn't very tall, his nose just so high,
Reaching edge of the table to smell a hot pie.

He knew if he touched with little grubby hand,
A long time in the corner he'd have to stand.
So standing on tiptoe, one eye guarding door,
He'd stretch just so far away from the floor.

Pink little nose, lifted high in the air,
His rosebud mouth tried a bite with great care.

We'd run in alarm when we'd hear his startled cry,
Oh, the pain of burned lip when tasting the pie.
We wouldn't have minded him taking a smell,
But he couldn't resist tasty bite as well.

Whenever you saw him with blister under nose,
You knew he'd been tasting on tippy toes.

Passing Rainbow

When day is done,
And it's evenings rest,
I think of the friends,
Of which I am blest.
I believe each is a messenger,
Bringing wisdom to my door.
Those who are rich in spirit,
Giving to a soul that's poor.
I gladly take from each who come,
Bearing gifts of enriching thought.
And different answers to life's battles,
For which I've dearly fought.
They leave a touch of humor,
Bits of wit and lots of love.
I know they must be guided,
By unseen power from above.
When my family and friends I visit,
And I'm welcomed into their home.
I hope I too, can leave a rainbow,
O'er a path of thought that they may roam.
May they be as richly blest as I,
With this passing rainbow in their sky.

Goodbye

Did you see the tear drops falling?
Did you feel the ache within my heart?
As I quietly kissed you on the cheek,
When for heaven you embarked.

Do you recall our angry confrontations?
That always ended in compromise,
Or our father-daughter secrets,
That brought such a twinkle to your eyes.

I feel your presence near me,
You're not so very far away.
I look forward to being together again,
When God chooses the day.

We'll laugh and sing, and hug and share,
Of all that's happened since you've been there.
Then tell the stories as we did of old,
In a land where streets are made of gold.

God's Radiance

A beam of Gods radiance,
Shines on me each day.
Keeps my heart uplifted,
Washes my cares away.
Softly ever caressing,
Wrapped within its grace.
Helps me not to stumble,
I walk a steady pace.
Strength to soul it gives,
A warmth deep within.
No cold can ever enter,
As I walk with Him.
A beam of Gods radiance,
Nothing can ever dim.

Compassion

One of the most enriching acts
Within this world of man,
Is to reach across a lonely space,
And lend a helping hand.
With cheerful countenance,
You must meet the rising dawn.
Ready and unassuming,
To do your best.
Give someone a rest,
Who is weary and deserving.
Watchful eyes
Will realize,
Blessings He'll bestow
Upon your life.
Because He knows
You really care,
And are compassionate enough,
To sympathize.

Revelation

A walk I took beside the brook,
To daydream and to ponder.
My life and ways, my ill-spent days,
And the necessity to wander.

I have a home, I'm not alone,
But loneliness invades me.
My heart unfilled, my life untilled;
Is this why happiness evades me?

No one would know which way I go,
If loneliness, I did not share.
So weak and weary, so bleak and dreary.
Isn't there anyone to care?

A voice, a song, He came along,
He touched my hand, He touched my heart.
The loneliness is gone.

MARIE E. McFADDEN

Mother's Comfort

The baby cried and the mother consoled,
Wiping each tear off the cheek it rolled.
Tenderly crooning she held it to breast,
There will be peace, you will find rest.

A toddler it grew, he learned how to walk.
Independent he became, he learned how to talk.
Carefully coaching and adding some weight,
His spirit grew strong, his body tall and straight.
Bravely, he treads down life's weary road,
Carrying the weight of each heavy load.
He seemed to remember when put to life's test,
There will be peace, you will find rest.

Tired and aged, one eve closed his eyes,
Quietly, he slept but he didn't arise,
Wafting silently upward, an angel he met.
Telling him gently, "You'll have no regret."
As the great gates were opened, he entered in,
There stood his mother to welcome him.
Arms enfolding him close to her breast.
He heard her whisper,
"You've found peace, you've found rest."

Eternities Wish

I see no silver rainbow,
No city streets paved in gold.
I want no pearled scepter,
Too costly for my hand to hold.
I don't ask for jewel studded sandals,
Or for a gown of purest white.
Nor for a crown upon my tresses,
That casts a brilliant light.

Dear God, if I were granted wishes,
If you could answer this peasant's dream,
Just give me an old log cabin,
Beside a clear mountain stream.

Let me sit in morning's stillness,
And watch the rising of the sun.
While I wonder in amazement,
At the work my God has done.
I would climb the mountains peak,
Taste the icy fallen snow.
I'd lay upon sweet smelling earth,
To watch a flower grow.
I'd listen to the secrets,
Whispered by the trees,
Or chase a painted butterfly.
Floating lightly on a breeze.
Let me keep the diamond droplets,
Spring showers sent to earth.
Triggering all the science,
Responsible for new birth.
Let me watch the changing seasons,
Like floats of a passing parade.
Painted with glorious colors,
That He has richly made.

I'd spend my days rejoicing,
All the beauty that He's created.
Thirst for peace and stillness,
Will never be abated.
Oh, what a heaven on earth,
He's already given to me;
It would be my wish for eternity.

Youth's First Love

Oh, golden Apollo,
Who came on wings of night.
Bringing forth a day from yesteryear,
While remembered youth prods my slumber.
With rays of searing light,
My soul strives to capture the scene.
Projected in my sleep, before it too quickly passes on,
For tomorrow memory will demand a recounting.
Of dreams before the dawn,
I'm again enraptured by the sight of you.
My quickened pulse taunts the heartbeat to go astray,
Unbound from realities chains.
My feet begin to dance, whirling, whirling,
To the music that you play.
Oh, golden Apollo,
Could I remember only summer's sun
Warming youths first precious love?
I need not touch the corner of your tender mouth,
Nor look for adulation from eyes of sky and sea.
For memory wrapped that special season,
Leaving it as a gift to me.
Visions long ago buried come to light.
The wrappings float gently to the ground.
A gaping wound, letting life's blood flow
Is there, where memories gift was bound.
No, my golden Apollo, I cannot forget,
The pain of youth's first love, nor, cease to hear
You, who comes on wings of night,
Bringing forth a day from yesteryear.

Written in Gold

Ah, riches have I in this land
Where people are sorely poor.
'Tis a fool that does not take the riches,
That are placed before him.
At no cost,
If fools would open their eyes,
They would not ask,
For more.

God gave riches
No money could buy.
Happiness, security, love,
And fools stand idly by,
Waiting for a fortune,
That will never come.

How long will you wait
To take God to heart?
Why not do it now
Like I?
Let God be your savior,
Let your name be on a cloud
In the sky,
Written in gold,
By God.

MARIE E. McFADDEN

A Christmas Tale

It isn't the whispers or the shouts of glee,
It isn't the mistletoe, nor, is it the tree.
Or presents and wrappings, or Christmas greetings,
Tinsel or lights, or late practice meetings.
It isn't the packages secured with twine,
Nor, is it the cards getting mailed on time.
It isn't getting done as quick as a wink,
It isn't St. Nick whose eyes had a twink.
It isn't the sewing or last stores run,
But to many, it's these things rolled into one.

Let's stop and think for a moment this year,
Just what it means to have Christmas cheer.
We wait until Easter for rebirth of nation,
Didn't it start, really, at a shepherd's station?
When one weary night a mother gave birth,
To a child who'd become king of the earth.
From heaven He was sent to teach us to love,
A star signaled the event in the sky up above.
Three wise men traveled spreading the tale,
No thoughts in their heads of thorn and nail.
But die on the cross He did for us all,
Paying the price when we stumble and fall.

Instead of our presents of glitter and gold,
Faith, hope, and charity are gifts to behold.
So give of yourself, learn the art of real living,
A time for real gifts and a time of true giving.
Help those less fortunate, ones tired and weary,
Put light in a life that's worn and dreary.
Remember God's blessings, start a happier year,
Give with your heart, spread peace and good cheer.

Weight of Tarnish

I saw him with a soul of purest gold,
Masculine beauty that God had made from a special mold.
Thoughtful, gentle, and patient, too.
Until occasion cast the glint of steel blue,
Finely forged with strength and pride,
Which added to the beauty of his manly stride.
Yet no robot of perfection hath God produced,
Within us all the devil can be loosed.
Was he aware? Had he seen or did he see?
Or unknowingly had he shown only me?
Life had left its ugly mark,
Raked across his eyes, a bright red spark,
That I had missed at first.
Cruelty could quench his angers thirst,
He bantered words with hammer practiced blow.
Driving deeply, knowing he could bruise the soul.
I felt life's ugliness as well,
Still wear the scars of a different hell.
Can love be strong enough to stand and hold?
The heavy weight of tarnish,
Found upon souls of purest gold?

Death

Oh, death you're no surprise to me.
Hurry, hurry towards my destiny.
Sad, maybe, how many sunrises,
Did I fail to see?
No matter, I remember one,
And, eve, when twilight brought the dark,
When day was done.

I've seen the birth of seasons,
Rocked babies on my knee.
Held fast a dying old man's hand.
Death, do you understand?
I know you for what you are,
Also, for what you'll be,
No, death, you're no surprise to me

Life is but a vapor that so quickly fades,
Would I trade?
Of course, death, because I've seen and heard,
The soaring of eagles, the song of a bird.
Death, you are hope and promise.
Aha! Did I surprise thee?
Quickly now, my Father awaits,
Hurry, hurry, toward my destiny.

MARIE E. MCFADDEN

Black Tide

The black tide rolls,
Entrapping its unwary prey.
In sparkling silver foam,
Erosive forces, rationalized.
By uncommitted spirits,
Eats away at proven foundations of time.

The black tide rolls,
Taking to its watery grave,
Honor, decency, esteem, truth.
Twisting it's slimy tentacles
In a choking death grip, all who go,
Too far, too fast, too long, towards
It's abysmal grasp.

The black tide rolls,
Above its thundering roar.
You can hear the screams
Of the dying soul and smell
The stench of fear or despair,
But look closer, listen, brave.

The black tide rolls,
Below the soft whispering air of spirit wings,
Snatching, quickly, uplifting, soothing,
touching, educating, supporting,
Those who gained favor with the great spirit,

The black tide rolls.

Ode to Beauty

Lest there be no trail winding,
Fir needled and spongy to my step.
On distant mountains,
With alpine meadows, glacial streams,
And tall timber heaven swept,
Or sandy beaches blessed with oceans,
Rolling surf of white and green.
Depositor of minute treasure,
Priceless only to me,
Found in soapy foam or marshy grass,
Upon a dune of timeless energy.
If vast desert of heat and stone,
No longer strives to show its worth,
Cradling cacti blooms and ages past,
When painted sky of dawn or setting sun,
Masks the beauty of this earth with darkness,
Let me pass quietly.

MARIE E. McFADDEN

It's Too Late

It's too late to watch the wood being cut,
From which the cross was made.
Too late to hold a palm leaf,
For which to give Him shade.
Too late to see the crown of thorns,
Piercing round His head.
While life's blood was flowing,
That for all mankind He shed.

But my friend, it's not too late
For all of us to know,
The cross of sin we share.
It's not too late to realize,
We're forgiven and protected,
Only by His loving care.
It's not too late for us to remember,
There was a reason for His death,
Or that in His tender mercy,
He gives us eternal breath.

Even though the pages of history
Will slowly pass away,
The scene of the Resurrection
Will endure until Judgment Day.

Fires in the Sky

It'll make no difference,
If you're a bum out in the cold,
Or wearing a top hat,
And rings of solid gold.
All the commuters will stop in traffics rush,
Even the crying babies will whimper then hush.
When they hear of the angels,
Lighting fires in the sky,
It'll be a whole new world, for you and I.

There'll be no more hatred,
Between the white and the black.
No more premonitions, when the earth is going to crack.
No more confusion, about a politicians way.
No more tapped phone calls, or taxes to pay.
When you hear of the angels,
Lighting fires in the sky,
It'll be a whole new world for you and I.

It'll be too late to question,
If you've done your very best.
Too late to go back, and repeat life's test.
It'll be time for the scoreboards,
To be tallied and shown.
Time to show, on this earth, how much you have grown.
When you hear of the angels,
Lighting fires in the sky,
It'll be a whole new world for you and I.

On Campus

Concrete walls and wearied halls,
Congealing thoughts of today.
Fostering dreams of tomorrow,
Impregnated by experience of yesterday.

Concrete walls and wearied halls,
Exchanging need for fulfillment.
Dreams for reality,
Satisfaction for inspiration.

Discipline?

I've heard it said, old fashioned discipline is dead.
That this is why our young are off the tracks,
And older folks say, all they really need today,
Are a few resounding old fashioned whacks.
You can take it from me, Mother never spared me.
The switch was always kept near at hand,
For the child who misbehaved, who was rude or depraved,
Or couldn't quite comply with her command.
The woodshed stood ready for a hand that was heavy,
And not just for the axe it would seem.
Though for wood it was used, I never was confused.
It stood ready for the kid who was mean.
Psychology played the hand, when a father took a stand;
About the respectful obedience of a child.
You knew you had no choice, though he didn't raise his voice;
For the lecture that was coming wouldn't be mild.
Remembering one day, when I didn't readily obey,
Mother said, "This child has really done a wrong."
"Father, you correct her and not with a simple lecture."
Oh, the trip to the woodshed was long.
While studying pile by the block, my knees began to knock;
And he chose a stick with precision.
Then while slapping his knee, he said gravely to me;
"I have made a definite decision."
You cry loud and clear for Mother she must hear,
And she'll think that my duty has been done.
No spanking did he give, but as long as I live,
My undying obedience he had won.
I remember to this day when my own go astray,
And I have to decide just which is right.
Old fashioned correction versus psychologies protection,
And the old woodshed and dad pops into sight.
I agree each kind is needed, but it was father I heeded;
And I really have to laugh at the thought.
Kids need a whack, old fashioned discipline they lack,
Remembering the spanking, I never got.

Nature's Voice

Oh, listen my children and you shall hear,
The growing grass, the running deer.
Upon your ear the sounds will fall,
Of the whispering trees, stalwart, tall.
The bird in the bush has its song to sing,
Their own orchestration the insects bring.
Babbling brook chatters endlessly,
Proclaiming its own odyssey.
Sun smiles warm from Father sky,
While whipped cream clouds go drifting by.
Assured you'll be, God's on His throne,
As Mother Earth tends her own.
Oh, listen my children and you shall hear,
God's gentle way of calming your fear.

MARIE E. MCFADDEN

Life's Mardi Gras

Tightly, the mask was fitted in its place,
He did not know his heart had etched its lines,
Wherefore, the mask had become his face.
Firmly hidden, he thought, from all the world to see,
Knowing not, she'd read each beating pulse, so easily.
Wounded deeply; untouchable; buried within his fears,
Yet she had felt his secret abilities for love and life,
Which undermined the wall she'd built with diligent stone,
Securely placed through passing years.

She had held the mask tightly in its place,
She did not know her heart had etched its lines,
Wherefore, the mask had become her face.
Daring not to give; afraid to pay the price of love.
Hidden, she thought from all the world to see,
Until, he'd reached out to her, so tenderly,
With his kind and gentle hand,
Revealing her who had, also held the mask,
Finding one, who could understand.

Worrisome

Baby:
I've waited so long,
But the wail is strong.
Angels watch from above,
I'll have to trust in all His love.
No need to worry.

Toddler:
The fevers so high,
Breath is but a sigh.
I hold her hand and bow in prayer,
She is His and He'll take care.
No need to worry.

Child:
First time to go away,
I must keep very busy today.
She seems so small yet unafraid,
What a beautiful child He has made.
No need to worry.

Teen:
First time on a date,
Not necessary for me to wait.
He has seen that she is ready,
I, too, fell in love with her steady.
No need to worry.

Young Adult:
Now I've sent her out alone,
Now she's on her very own.
Is He with her taking care?
Will He always be right there?
Now, I worry.

Hidden Strength

Oh, weary body,
That's known the sleepless night.
Babies cries and restless sleep,
'Til dawn's early light.
Days of sorrow, faults, and lonely fears.

Oh, weary body,
Had I remembered this,
I'd never reached these many years.

If I'd never had time to see,
Apple blossoms upon the tree.
Not seen the elk in the cranberry bog,
Ne'er heard the blue grouse,
Thumping on his log.

If I'd never remembered skies of blue,
Sweet hay, camping fires, and morning's dew.
If I hadn't looked up, down, all around,
With eyes that were free and clear.

Oh, weary body,
Had I not remembered this,
I'd not reached these many years.

Marie E. McFadden

Samaritan in the Bar

Why here? I ask myself,
Touched by deeper thought.
'Tis not a place of choice,
For better, I have fought.
Twirling ice, around the glass,
The cherry bobs up and down.
Perhaps, I'll loose the devil,
Meaning the angel has to drown.
Circumstance has pushed me,
Now fate must cast its spell.
Only but an easy forward step,
To unlock the gates of hell.

What holds this night? I ask,
When interrupted by a voice of gentle strain.
Then gliding in the arms of a stranger,
Possessing strength only tall men can retain.
Somehow, as if by diligent practice,
Their steps fittingly coincide.
Like wind billowing sails of a ship,
Floating softly on the tide.
Maybe for a lofty moment,
The essence of a dream I'll hold.
Until the mornings stillness,
Is dashed with realities bitter cold.
Once fates clutching grasping hand has lost,
Again I've taken my command.
Placed by a cautious stranger,
Safe-footed and sure on solid land.

A Choice

There are two paths
That lead through life,
One is wrong
One is right.

There's none between
That we might wander,
So do not tarry
Or dare to ponder.

For if we ourselves
Make a path to follow,
In life's despair
We're sure to wallow.

Keep to the path
That's sure and true,
The one God made
Just for you.

Depression

Too late to run the fields of green,
Or walk through storms at night.
Daring lungs to burst with air,
Unafraid of thunders roll and lightning's bolt of white.

It's too late to laugh at nothing,
Or to make a dream your private treasure.
Too late to watch a summers moon
Pave a silver path across the sea,
While the beauty of the night wraps my soul in ecstasy.

Too late, too late, my heart doth cry,
When unlocking the door to memories past.
Shut it quickly, turn quietly away,
Lest you hurt too deeply within its grasp.

Too late to wonder why I chose this path,
Closed in darkness, to steep and rough to climb.
Or why I gave my life to one,
Who cast no warmth of sunlight to give me peace of mind.

Much too late to look for roses,
When the bouquet holds only thorns.
Too late to sail into a tranquil inlet,
When all your life has been spent in storms,
It's too late, much too late.

*****

From *Webster's Dictionary*, a definition that I related to most closely was the word heartsick. I was sick of the abuse, the loss of my worth, and suicide was against my beliefs, however, not discounted. I found there is help, there is someone who understands, there are many who care. Please, find the courage to make just one phone call.

1-800-562-6025
Washington Domestic Violence Hotline

A Thought to a Sponsor

What do I ask of thee, my friend,
When I seek only my needs of today?
Just someone to share a moment, an hour
While I gropingly search my own way.
May I borrow your strength, your warmth, your hope;
Without invading your space in time?
'Tis not my intention to burden thee,
Only to ease this encumbrance of mine.

Marie E. McFadden

The Dishrag

Don't be tied to Ma's apron strings, son.
Get on a track and run, run, run.
Dis is what folks done tel', baby brother.
Sure wisht I were a boy, steada tother.
It's most enough to make me gag,
Cause I got tied to the damn dishrag.

Dat ole rag made me late fer a date,
'enny thin' excitin', and I didn't rate.
An ole piece o' flannel, er unnerpants,
Times I hid it, thinkin' jist by chance.
Da dishes might disappear, maybe fer good,
But ma al'ays foun' it and said girls should.
Darn dat rag, when bruther was outside,
I was at de sink and was dishrag tied.

Times it'd stink and get slimy an' sour,
A cleanun' be hung, waitin' fer de hour.
Fer stacks o' dishes to be done,
If I 'twas a boy, I'd run, run, run.

But jist like a girl, I done got wed,
Deres dishes all day, an' after goin' off to bed.
Doan make a matter if' n it's pretty or not.
I hope de one who made de dishrag,
Is where it's mighty HOT.

Riddle

Seven sparkling diamonds,
Untouched by man.

Timeless space,
I'll never span.

Gloriously brilliant,
For all to see.

Much more than your name,
You are to me.

What am I?

The big dipper.

MARIE E. McFADDEN

Prayer Is a Start

The night was cold, the sky gone dim,
I wondered if I could call on Him.
I wondered if He could-but no, it's too late.
I'll hurry on, not hesitate.
So stumbling on, in deep despair,
I thought that life had been unfair.
I had to end this lonely life,
That held so much trouble, so much strife.
I tried to jump, but tripped and fell,
In my soul, I saw the depths of hell.
I got to my knees and began to cry,
Oh Lord, help me! I don't want to die.
Take my hand and hold it tight,
Lead me on with glory bright.
The words just tumbled out, straight from the heart,
I knew this was the beginning, for prayer is a start.

My Lovin' Mate

The past half hour, I've fairly run.
But the table's set and dinner's done.
Coffee's perked and turned on low,
Kids are quiet, watchin' a TV show.
Sittin' in my favorite chair? Well, no,
Whether there's sun, rain, sleet, or snow.
At 5:30 PM each day of the week,
When the homeward bound, has reached its peak.
Across from the Warta, in my car I await,
My lovin' mate.

I sit quietly and think of this long day,
Takin' care of six kids and a house ain't hay.
I haven't had time to give father a thought,
Other than to remember, he likes his dinner hot.
Now, I'll try to be cheerful and remember to smile,
The things that went wrong, can just wait for a while.
The broken window, the hole in the wall,
Maybe I'll forget to tell him at all.
No sense temptin' the hand of fate, or
My lovin' mate.

Now, buses and crummies start comin' down the street
Bringin' tired out crews, we wives come to meet.
Hickorys, snagged pants, nosebags, tin hats; corks tied together.
Caked on mud, just a sign of behind the cat or bad weather.
They all look alike until you see their faces,
As they all pass by to find their right places.
Here comes one and I nod just to be polite,
But it turns out to be the one I take home at night.
This is the only time I can be sure of a date with,
My lovin' mate.

Marie E. McFadden

A Rose

Swirled rubies and garnets,
Startling gold,
Multi-colors midst green unfold.
Gems to twinkle the eye,
Fragrance taunting the nose,
Known only to God and man,
As a rose.

Tulips

Pink, red, and yellow fluted cups,
Filled with droplets of spring rain.
I wonder if angels sip your sweet nectar,
While we dream in gentle slumber.

Fall

Frost is on the pumpkin,
Fog wraps the earth.
Everything is dying,
We wait through winter's death,
For springs glorious rebirth.

Marie E. McFadden

Sharing Love

We forgot the day,
And the sun so bright.
We forgot the moon,
And the starry night.
We had no troubles, we had no cares.
We just had a love,
We had to share.

The world walked by,
And so did time.
They smiled at each other,
And said, "It's fine,
The way two hearts, in love always fair."
They knew too,
We had a love to share.

Life went on with things to do,
There was always time
To whisper, "I love you."
God kept us happy,
For He heard our prayer.
He knew too,
We had a love to share.

Sunset

Clouds lazily drift,
In a pattern above.
Casting a pink glow,
O'er the land I love.

Day is now done,
Shadows come dim.
The sun slowly sets,
O'er horizons far brim.
Our dreams are protected,
The sun begins to fade.
Leaving a rosary sunset,
That God has made.

In Hiding

Dare I tear down this secure wall I've built,
Protecting my soul and pride?
Dare I let suns warm rays seep through,
To melt the ice inside?
Dare I let him know how vulnerable I can be,
Lest he wield a striking blow?
Locking again my heart from reality,
Oh, dear God, he could not know.

Dare I put away life's game of hide and seek,
Hiding my heart, seek not the faithful years.
Afraid to share, to love, to give,
For me there's been only hurt and tears.
Day by day and year by year,
Each stone was placed with care,
Carefully covering life's iniquities,
Which were too great to bear.
Thinking the spring gone dry,
Leaving nothing but arid riverbed.
Fate swung its withered wand my way,
Creating a new fountainhead.

Dare I tear down the wall,
Letting life's rushing waters flow?
Would I drown or could I set sail again?
Oh, dear God, I do not know.

Marie E. McFadden

Stacy's Stick

We'd waited through long winter,
Now summer was at our door.
We happily began packing,
All our bedding, clothes and store.
We were off to alpine meadows,
Of leisure, sun and shade.
We would set about our pleasures,
As soon as camp was made.

First day dawned bright and shining,
We chose our path with care.
For, behind us would be tagging,
Sleepy eyes with straggling hair.
They seemed to stagger and stumble,
Like they needed a helping hand.
So Father found each a walking stick,
Along bubbling brook, where glaciers ran.

The baby was four and now enthused,
Her stick she enjoyed and thoroughly used,
For poking in holes, or disturbing a bug,
Splashing in water, or in dirt she dug.
She drug it behind or pushed it in front,
Not seeming to acquire the trick,
Or learning to master the articulate art
Of hiking with a walking stick.

She used it to clobber a partner,
Whenever her anger they roused.
Or chased a scurrying chipmunk,
To wherever his food was housed.
Along the road, she pecked and scraped,
Like fingernails on blackboard in school.
With teeth on edge, nerves grated raw,
Despised was the one who'd invented this tool.

But she never parted with stick in hand,
And we hiked for eight miles long.
Only way to close out the noise of the stick,
Was to burst into rollicking song.
With strength wearing out,
She seemed smaller than her pack.
Tightening her grip on the stick,
She hitched rides piggy-back.

Back to camp we finally arrived,
And took a long needed rest.
A sleepy little girl, held fast to a stick,
That proved a friend, when put to the test.
Along cabin wall,
It stood when not needed.
Her threatening voice not to touch,
We carefully all heeded.
No better friend could father pick,
Than summers very first,
Walking stick.

Days Beginning

I've made the beds, the start of my chores,
Swept and scrubbed all of my floors.
Disinfected the bath and washed the walls,
Cleaned the stairs and dusted the halls.
The kitchen stands all sparkling clean,
All cracks have been scraped in between.
Front room is vacuumed, boy, it was a sight.
No sign of the struggle it had last night.
Trash has been emptied, the laundry put in.
Now it's 10 AM,
Time for my day to begin.

Mother

I can remember, at the sewing machine one night,
Your face looked tired in the kerosene light.
But I didn't notice and had to be told,
Take care, my dear,
Mothers get old.

Once you pinned pink blossoms in your hair,
I thought you the most beautiful everywhere.
I didn't notice and had to be told,
Take care, my dear,
Mothers get old.

God's angel came down from heaven one day,
He painted your hair a silvery gray.
But I didn't notice and had to be told,
Take care, my dear,
Mothers get old.

Even though your hair turned gray,
You never changed in anyway.
I didn't notice and had to be told,
Take care, my dear,
Mothers get old.

MARIE E. McFADDEN

My Son

I know not what this child might face,
Whatever he must, I pray with grace.
Would that his strength, unlike Goliaths might,
Give him hope and wisdom, with David's insight.
When winds of life buffet and bow his back,
May he strive onward, on with the attack.
If he has learned the price of pride and greed,
After God has finished guiding his deeds.
And he's successfully walked in the world of men,
Then, and only then,
Knowing not where this child must roam,
But for a time, I'd wish him here back home.

MARIE E. MCFADDEN

Logger Poem

I can remember a long time ago,
My dad, we'd go to meet.
I can see the speeder comin' down the track,
My dad, he'd look worn and beat.
So I promised then when I was eight,
I'd never make such a bad mistake,
As marryin' a logger.

After stompin' brush and jumpin' logs,
From six to six that day.
He still had hours of milkin' cows,
Feedin' chickens and pitchin' hay.
So I promised then when I was eight,
I'd never make such a bad mistake,
As marryin' a logger.

Once when winter was mighty bad,
And the snow was three feet deep.
I saw my dad come home one night,
With hands froze blue,
And chunks of ice for feet.
So I promised then when I was eight,
I'd never make such a bad mistake,
As marryin' a logger.

I saw him sick with pneumonia and colds,
Muscles pulled and broken bones.
He fought for work and laid off on strikes,
And cussed and swore in heavy tones.
So I promised then when I was eight,
I'd never make such a bad mistake,
As marryin' a logger.

Well, I met a sailor home from the sea,
Who was looking for a new vocation.
We said, "I do" and settled down.
Then, I was in a helluva situation.
For I'd promised me when I was eight,
I'd never make such a bad mistake,
As marryin' a logger.

He learned to stomp, brush, and jump on logs,
And finally ended up as a hooker.
On a Friday night, he straddles a stool,
With more steam than a pressure cooker.
So I promised my daughters,
When they were eight,
They couldn't make such a bad mistake,
As marryin' a logger.

Lonely Doesn't Have to Be Forever

Lonely doesn't have to be forever,
Everyday doesn't have to be so blue.
Lonely doesn't have to be forever,
If you accept the fact that someone loves you.
You've had more than your share of troubles and tears in your eyes,
You've had too many heartbreaks and heard too many lies.

But lonely doesn't have to be forever,
Because every woman isn't untrue.
Lonely doesn't have to be forever,
If you accept the fact that I really love you.
I can change your world,
Where no tears have to fall.
And we could be happy if you care for me at all,
Lonely doesn't have to be forever.

Memories Are Mine

Be sure the second time around,
Wait three years and prove your ground.
As long as doubt stands in your way,
Wait some more for a better day.
But alas, to all who sin,
The miracle of birth calls within.
It was a farce from the start,
He could not give from the heart.
I kept his house and kept his bed,
While he filled our life with fear and dread.
Two mistakes, He'll not forgive,
This is the way that you must live.
Try until death is sweet,
Then rebel, then retreat.
Close the door, shed no more tears,
Just exist and count the years.
Ne'er once did God forget,
Nor loosed my clinging hand.
He gave me strength and my children's love,
So alone I could always stand.
Awakening one day I screamed at the sky,
Let me live or let me die.
What 'ere the price I'm going to pay,
So, show me one more sunny day.
Fill my days with answered dreams,
Let tears of joy flow free.
For all that was forbidden,
Has now been granted me.
Ah, but payments due with interest,
The collector stands nearby.
'Tis time to pay for screaming,
Let me live or let me die.
One thing I shall not relinquish,
The memories are mine to own.
They are the priceless jewels I carry,
As once more I stand alone.

Marie E. McFadden

Oh, Heavy Laden

Come, ye who are heavy laden,
Come, and I'll give you rest.
Oh, Lord were I worthy,
Enough to be blest.

Despair descending upon my soul,
My vision clouded obscuring my goal.
Physically unable to loosen my bonds,
Only a command could make me respond.
Imprisoned by failing emotions,
Devoid of all prayerful devotions;
My spirit starving and depressed,
Come, ye who are heavy laden,
Come, and I'll give you rest.

A lift, a light, inspired insight,
A golden ray in darkest night.
A prayer of hope, a helping hand,
Within my hell I heard a command.
Replenished soul, I have been blest.
Come, ye who are heavy laden,
Come, I'll give you rest.

A Pause

I tuck them into bed at night,
Give each a kiss, turn out the light.
Thank goodness it's over, I say to myself,
Then, take a good book down from the shelf.

I get all settled in my easy chair,
Run a tired hand through disarrayed hair.
Give a sigh of relief that the day is done,
Now, I'm up and on the run.

"I got to go bathroom, I want a drink,"
Each one has got to say.
I know that I was foolish to think,
That this was the end of the day.

Within My World

Within my world of darkness and light,
I try to achieve an honest insight.
Facing reality with accurate understanding,
Following chosen path unmeandering.
Let me find through laughter or tears,
Strength to sustain me through the years.
Though darkness might my vision dim,
Let the light of goodness guide me to Him.
With trials assailing and fate unaltered,
I'm sure He knows my faith never faltered.
When this pathway has been tread at last,
Let me not feel shame for time that has past.
May each treasured moment given today,
Be a blessing for tomorrow and Judgment Day.

Marie E. McFadden

Pronunciation

Oh, got a bruise, got a bite,
Just not feeling right.
Here, have some of Stacy's num-num.

Oh, cat has a scratch,
He's not your match.
Here, give him Stacy's num-num.

Oh, poor dolly's got the flu,
Or are you just feeling blue.
Here, have some Stacy's num-num,

It'll cure your ills,
Doesn't add to your bills.
Whatever your ailment,
It's sure to denounce.
Mentholatum is num-num,
To babes who can't pronounce.
Here, have some Stacy's num-num.

Reverie of Fall

Maple leaves, turned red and gold,
Jack Frost had painted fall.
Companionship kindled cozy warmth,
Within the cabin small.
Two friends relaxed amiably,
Light banter filled the air.
Aloud they dreamt of hunting,
Or thought of maidens fair.
Quiet peace enclosed the room,
From my lips escaped a sigh
As I remembered long ago,
Sweet evenings like this gone by.

Kerosene lamps cast shadows,
While I watched the embers glow.
Curled beside the old wood heater,
Listening to mens talk, softly flow.
It was a secure feeling,
You knew all was going well.
When they easily talked of farming,
Or were giving logging hell.

Tobacco smoke curled upward,
Rolling their own from a Bulldurham sack.
Yes, it was a very pleasant evening,
That I spent at Lester's shack.

The Brighter Side

Today, mirth will girdle me,
Against the cares of the world.
Laughter rippling from my depths,
Like all nations flags unfurled.
Yesterday tears were shed,
And heavy was my yolk.
Today I'll not remember,
It was my heart that broke.
Humor shall entrap me,
Cheer I'll spread with love.
My way shall be lighted,
By angels from above.
We're surely blest to have a choice,
When each new dawn is made.
For His spirit reinforces our faith,
Whenever it begins to fade.

Beyond

Soul's separation,
Lifting, wafting free.
Contemplation,
Drawn to voice unheard.
Draft, space less, uncolored white,
Timeless, yet familiar.
Had I traveled here before?
Perhaps in birth,
Or another age.

Two hands of love and tenderness extended,
A voice, compassionate, profound.
Come nigh hand, release be found,
Defer, entreat, unfinished work,
Reversion, but promised yet.

An act to perform, teach believing,
I know not death, but a part of living.
Fear not a friend,
Waiting.

Wisdom's Gentle Nudging

Wisdom's gentle nudging,
Said keep the door unopened.
Yet I had too quickly seen,
That little boy glee;
Escaping from his eyes.

Wisdom's gentle nudging,
Said keep the door unopened.
But I hesitated to long,
To miss the hungry warmth;
Deep blue like summers skies.

Wisdom's gentle nudging,
Said keep the door unopened.
Though his touch excitedly,
Quietly reminded me of;
Some buried forgotten need.

Wisdom's gentle nudging,
Said keep the door unopened.
And I wanted to hear,
Nature's insistent manipulation;
Activating loves planted seed.

So be gone with you wisdom,
I want to feel, touch, hear, and see.
I am aware of risk, heartbreak, loss,
For this space in time I want this.
Whatever the ending will be,
Wisdom means wise.
I turn my back,
A bit of me dies.

Forward

Will I ever again recapture
The peace that comes with dawn?
Will I spend an evening quietly
While dreams go marching on?
Will there be uninterrupted moments
When time is all I own?
Will I be left with just a house
When once I had a home?

If I've spent my life in giving,
But now set back and take.
There'll be many unopened gifts,
That are left beside my gate.

I don't think I'd like the idea,
Growing old and empty handed.
Or, being cast upon a peaceful isle,
Alone and there left stranded.

I've decided not to recapture,
The peace that comes with dawn.
With my grandchildren's approval,
I'll help their dreams march on.

Sunday Afternoon

It was a lazy Sunday,
I decided to take my ease.
We drove to the neighborhood drive in,
I said order what you please.
With food devoured I paid the bill,
And raised my shake cup for a toast.

The cost would have been much cheaper,
If we stayed home eating a sirloin roast.

All across the country,
On a Sunday afternoon.
The drive in lot is crowded,
And you pay the pipers tune.
With burgers, fries, and shake,
The public sure is blest.

Someone to cook Sunday dinner,
While we take a Sunday rest.

Spring's First Robin

Black wing, red breast,
Faithful tender of the nest.
I can't imagine an early spring,
Without the beauty of which you sing.
Waking us at break of dawn,
Gathering breakfast from our lawn.
Scolding us like a stranger,
When you think your young in danger.
Black wing, red breast,
I'd like you to remember.
I'm the landlord,
You're the guest.

Not Too Big and Not Too Tall

Would that I could keep her small?
Not too big and not too tall.
Would that I could always see?
Those snapping black eyes peering up at me,
Long pigtails flying, voice resounding against the sky.
A great big package of "no can do's and I can't try."

Pockets full of wiggly things,
From worms and moths and yesterday's bug.
She can't resist as she passes the cat,
To grab its tail in a friendly tug.

You can't believe one word you're told,
With every inch she grows, she gets more bold.

All dressed up in Sunday's best,
She acts like she's supposed to do,
Until she starts pulling up knee socks,
Or scratching her leg with the toe of her shoe.

From sister's drawers she collects her treasure,
To hear them scream gives her pleasure.

Fiend and monster, savage and beast,
All of these to say the least.
But when she's bathed and fast asleep,
She's just that age I'd like to keep.

Would that I could keep her small,
Not too big and not too tall.

Brad

Lest you think my air be light,
My voice empty and of brassy sound.
Take a trip with me through words,
Where my inner thoughts abound.

Though I'm positive in my beliefs,
And from faith I'll never stray.
His going unleashed emotions,
Putting doubt in knowing's way.

Memory hears a tender whisper,
"My Marie" falls on listening ears.
Remembering impish smiles,
I brush away escaping tears.
For while clouds shall drift across sureties empty sky,
Comes reasons understanding sunshine;
Again on you and I.

He is with God.

Brad was my friend's son and we shared a special bond. He was my son's best friend. Many hours were spent at our house in play and friendship. Brad and I shared the same birthday. He never forgot to include me in his. On an elk-hunting trip, swerving to miss an elk on the road, the car ended in a creek where Brad drowned. I will always be able to hear him call me, "My Marie."

To the Little Child within Us All

Oh, little child,
I hear your cry.
Let me wipe away that tear.
Though you are grown,
All on your own,
Please know that I am here.

I will take care of you,
Today you can rely on me.
For I am growing, I am learning,
To be who I want to be.
I'll nurture and care for you,
Share my smile when you have
None of your own.
Just know, little child, deep within,
That I am here,
You are no longer alone.

Flowers

They spring up from their patchwork quilt of earth,
Straight and proud, joyous with their birth.
Sunbeams dance around their tiny heads,
To warm long cold winters bed.

A tinkling baby laugh, a faltering step,
It wasn't long until disaster they met.
We'll seed again and wait until spring,
And, pick them then when robins sing.

MARIE E. MCFADDEN

The Moon

Silver sphere,
With eyes of gloom.
Casting moonbeams,
Around my room.
'Causes me to creep from bed,
To watch from my window,
At the magic you've spread.

Life and Death of a Tree

Once it stood with arms in the sky,
Then came the saw and it was doomed to die.
Once it stood in silent prayer,
Now, it's felled without a care.

There with a cable around its neck,
It's drawn through the brush and dirt.
With taller trees peering down at it,
How could its pride go unhurt.

Then, a little guy not more than three,
Never knowing it had been a tree.
There was such a gleam in the little guy's eye,
That the tree shed all remorse.
No longer was it a plain old tree,
But a little guy's rocking horse.

Child's Winter

Howling wind like tigers loosed,
Prowled through the stormy night.
Surprised we were on awakening,
To find such an awesome sight.
Snow in swirling drifts,
Left the world while in its darkness lay.
A fairy land of frosty white,
Designed for a child at play.

Without the heart of a child,
Full of wriggling anticipation.
Snow becomes a heavy burden,
Beyond our wildest expectation.
They don boots and mittens,
Wrap woolen scarves about their necks.
Then play in a beautiful wonderland,
While our nerves are made a wreck.

Fuel bills are shooting skyward,
Chains are purchased for the car.
Shovels are heavier than remembered,
And we begin our winter war.
Fetch the candles, fill the larder,
Only emergency trips are planned.
Keep in touch with Mr. Weather,
TV and papers are thoroughly scanned.

Oh, for the heart of a child,
Whose happiness is ecstatic,
When snow flurries are flying,
When the sleds and woolies,
Are brought from the attic.
Yes, snow belongs to a child.
Their hearts filled with glee,
Instead of like me, going wild,
Counting the costs to me.

Marie E. McFadden

Fiftieth Wedding Anniversary for Mom and Dad

"What's forever, Jack?"
Perhaps, good, and bad in equal measure.
With God's hands molding love and care,
Giving fifty golden years of treasure.

I remember, through love and joy,
Hope and trust, something got mingled.
With anger, hate, disgust,
Then, standing at the doubters end,
Not knowing what's beyond the bend.

"I don't know what forever is, Bessie.
I remember your eyes of precious blue,
And hair as black as the raven's wing.
Oh, how you made my heart sing.
Then, in crept fear, self-hate, and sorrow.
I did not think there'd be a tomorrow."

Don't pay me no mind, I'm just a child,
With awkward legs and hair swept wild.
But I saw, yep, I saw my father there on bended knee,
Speaking to the one who walks with me.
And Mom, my mom in all her grown up ways.
I saw her with head bent in prayer,
Asking my friend to care.
Now, don't pay me no mind, I'm but a child,
But then, my grandma says I'm quite sly.
Seems to me something didn't die,
Parents most of all should know,
How hard it is to grow.
Look at me, trying to talk,
The troubles I took learning to walk.

And some of my friends with fat and dimples,
Knobby knees, freckles, and pimples,
And my sister's boyfriend found another,
And what about putting up with baby brother?

Growing is pain, but to me it's all a game.
After all, I'm but a child."

As she grew, she watched them grow,
Saw that they came to know.
He who blesses all endeavor,
He who answers, "What is forever?"

Today's Technology

GPS my way, oh Lord,
For oft I go astray.
Only disillusionment do I feel,
When I wander from your way.

GPS my way, oh Lord,
Man's technology is not enough direction.
To guide me down life's rocky road,
While giving me spiritual protection.

GPS my way, oh Lord,
I need thee, every day.
You and you alone can
Hear me when I pray.

Christmas Story

Christmas lights flicker,
So bright, so quick,
Children quietly whisper,
"Where is St. Nick?"
Supposedly sleeping,
Tucked into bed.
They wait for the reindeer,
With bright nose of red.

Sleigh bells jingling,
They sound so near.
Cocoa for Santa,
Carrots for reindeer.

Knock at the door,
The stomping of feet.
Grandparents with presents,
Beat a hasty retreat.

It's all a charade,
It's father's ho-ho.
The children all giggle,
The story they know.

Marie E. McFadden

The Key

I locked the door to my world,
Long ago, I threw away the key.
I wouldn't take a chance,
There was no first or second glance.
I'd locked the door to my world,
No one could hurt me, and then
You came along.
There was no place to hide,
Now it's open to be hurt again.

Your love warmed up my heart,
Melted all the ice away.
You turned all the nightmares
Into a sunny day.
You say you love me,
Then don't hurt me.
I don't want a lock on my world,
Just throw away the key.

My Apple Tree

I'm going to sit forever,
Perched high up in my tree,
Watching clouds in summer's sky,
Creating pictures just for me.

Wrapped in apple blossoms,
Their smell tantalizingly sweet.
Listening to the bee's orchestration,
While the Master times the beat.

I'll never leave my hideaway,
Far from the world of woes.
I'll stay up on its' mighty branch,
Imprisoning youth and wiggling sandy toes.

We'd all like to recapture a moment,
From time that too quickly passed away.
So hidden amongst the leaves and blossoms,
In my apple tree, I'm going to stay.

Marie E. McFadden

Wipe Away My Tears

I sought His face,
At the end of every day.
To thank Him for walking with me,
Each step I took this way.

I saw Him knelt on bended knee,
In the garden of Gethsemane.
I saw the tears rolling down His cheeks,
So I asked myself,
Of what worth are you and I?
How could we make
Our dear savior cry?

I prayed, dear God forgive;
Thank you, for giving us a chance to repent.
And for giving us renewed strength to try,
When our own strength is spent.
One day I'll wipe those tears away,
As He'll wipe mine on Judgment Day.

And There Were Seven

And there were seven,
Sent from heaven.
And there were seven,
And the house was full of love.
And there were seven,
Sent from heaven.
And there were seven,
Protected with His love.

Oh Lord, on bended knee I pray,
Keep watch o'er them-keep them safe today.
A mother's love must be strong,
A mother's faith must be long.

And there were seven,
Sent from heaven.
And there were seven,
Who didn't ask which way to go.
And there were seven,
Sent from heaven.
'Cause their momma said,
There's only one way you know.

Even though they might stray,
On bended knee I'll still pray.
A mother's love must be strong,
A mother's faith must be long.

And there were seven,
Sent from heaven.
And there were seven,
Six girls and one boy.
And there were seven,
And the house was full of joy.

The Twilight Hour

'Tis a time to rest,
Count your blessings.

No need for jingling coin,
Nor fancy dressings.

'Tis a time to know,
Wealth is health,
Health is wealth.

"Tis a season of a man's life,"
To relax.
To look back on dreams,
Wondering at these.

To quietly listen,
To whispering trees.

Take a walk,
Admire a flower.
Rest.

Let each day be spring,
Enjoy peace.
In our twilight hour.

Work had been life's vial of hope,
Climbing every hour
To success's door.
Now, 'tis time to rest,
For the mountain is gone.

"Tis time to wonder,"
For what we fought.

The reward of years,
We know not yet.
But it awaits,
In life's ending sunset.

The twilight hour.

Random Thoughts

How much our life is like a garden?
Wherein the flowers grow.
We nurture, fertilize, and weed,
Before the seed we sow.
We must clear the sad, shake out the chaff,
Dry our tears and learn to laugh.
Always searching for God's wisdom,
To feed our soul.

I have no aspiration,
For the sound of many hands.
Nor for royal recognition,
From distant foreign lands.

Greatness and I have no rapport,

If I can, but, bring a smile,
Or cease a tear,
To a friend or stranger,
Maybe, God will notice,
Remember my name;
Herein, will lie my fame.

We do not know how fast the world,
'Til we cross that dividing line.
Where little boys are changed to men,
And we walk in step with time.

When you've got troubles,
When you're sad and poor.
Forget thyself,
Lend a hand next door.

Last Words of Faith

A child is born and all rejoice,
Each strives to impart some intellectual teaching.
Yet never speak of the meaning of death,
For their own fear they'd rather the child
Never had to meet wicked hand reaching.
Unspoken word, death,
The heart cringes, heads lower,
Casting down their eyes,
They send pleading prayers for protection,
Winging toward the skies.
Fearing the unknown or death as deepest blackness,
Hiding within themselves, daring not to speak,
In open, unless with deliberate rashness,
Being bold or careless, even callous,
About their dying,
They laugh or cry or show fear.
Making a cover for an act that cannot be changed,
Knowing in so doing, beforehand it's been all arranged.
Accepting the beauties of life and blessings,
A babies smile, or spring meadows bursting with bloom.
They face trials with bravery or lose,
Convinced somehow they've won,
Stumbling on toward death as doom.
Half acceptable is death to one whose life has
Been fulfilled, still turn from thoughts that our turn awaits.
Harder yet to understand a babe who's laid to rest,
Plucked from loving mother's breast, when tiny fluttering
Heart has been stilled. Unprepared and full of doubts,
They meet their fate. Death.

Epilogue

It's I, who doesn't understand their thoughts,
The ugliness of death nor can accept
The sorcerer who blindly strikes,
Only beauty, friends, and painless peace,
With tender loving care,
A merciful god and forgiveness for me,
Are waiting where,
Others only darkness see.
Oh, blinding light and gentle hands,
The plan of life my God commands,
That in death I may find my rest.

If in His arms the young may lay,
Or about the edge of His garment play.
From this world's rendering pain may I be removed,
And upon His promise lie,
May I find only beauty to look forward to,
Upon the day I die,
Perhaps, in the moment of grief.
Doubts and fears might also assail me,
If in death a child removed,
Clouded my vision, so I could not see,
The beauty of which I speak, may my prayers too,
Be received, and the thoughts that death,
Is a reward of beauty to the living,
Be returned to me.

Writings

Camping by Trial and Error

"Frederick!" I screamed, "You're standing in the eggs!"

More hungry than sorry, my cousin paced around the campfire. Soon, one leg was longer than the other due to accumulated egg yolk, river sand, and alder twigs.

The morning wasn't going well at all. We'd slept out all night in rolled-up blankets and dew-damp pillows.

As the first light of dawn touched the sky, we moved indoors. Knowing Father would have a roaring fire in the cook stove. Warm and toasted, we gathered supplies for an outdoor breakfast on the riverbank.

While my brother and another cousin chased spawning salmon up the river, Fred and I had set about the camp chores. The fire was burning well, and so did the toast. I soon discovered when food is cooked; it should be placed on rocks close to the fire or on the back of the grate. That is if you had one, which we didn't.

Cook potatoes before eggs, because they take a longer time to cook. Cut very thin or they take forever. The family dog had his breakfast first. He stole the ham, while I helped Fred clean his heels.

Repeating Hiawatha and remembering the pictures of the succulent trout frying in father's men's magazines, I mentally made note of each mistake. I vowed that one day I'd master the art of camping and I'd make it fun.

Years of trial and error followed. Camping trips were made with aunts, uncles, and cousins into the mountains, to the beaches, or just in our own backyard. Being raised on an undeveloped homestead, which lay in the bend of the river, proved an excellent training ground. It was the early years of World War II and a lot of my camping experience derived from Junior Commando exercises we practiced each day. Each outing needs a commander, be it the father, mother, or teen with vital knowledge of leadership.

Father's work is more demanding in the summer. Yet seeing he needs to teach the children about outdoor survival, I became commander. Even if you've had no previous commando training, don't become discouraged. A mother raising small children automatically becomes first class material. Your duties will consist of the same trials you encounter on a weekend with the whole family at home.

A passable commander becomes top sergeant, who organizes a team of efficient workers. No one is exempt from duty, unless they're under walking age. The best character assets are a good sense of humor followed by patience. Camping is fun and its main purpose is to relax frayed nerves of everyday living. Keep this as your main objective. While everyone is enjoying themselves, you can slip in botany, biology, geography, psychology, archeology, astronomy, and many more. You must be in charge of supplies, clothing store, recreation equipment, and budget. You are head advisor of the planning committee, the health director, and avid woodsmen. It is to your advantage if you are familiar with highways and maps, park management, auto mechanics, weather, and first-aid.

Your first concern is budget. Raising seven children, I've always had concern for budget. Many families miss the fulfilling experience of camping because they envision great cost. With careful planning ahead, it can be done on a shoestring. Our most recent excursion took us into the Olympic Mountains. We spent an exciting week of swimming, hiking, side trips to museums, and points of interest. The expenses for the week were $91.73, and included a small cabin, five days of pool privileges, gas, oil, color film, souvenirs, two meals dining out, groceries that had to be bought fresh each day, spending money for the children, plus some added equipment. This was for two grown-ups and five children between the ages of fifteen and four.

Transportation needn't be too important, our only requirement being reliable. This is why, with expenses in mind, we chose an older station wagon with good tires, brakes, and a proven carburetor. It can be used for added sleeping space if one gets rained out during the night, also. We have made many trips with seven children, and found them to have sufficient room. Using finesse of a perfect hostess it's all in the seating of the guests to have rapport. Slightly more difficult in a two door intermediate compact, but the large trunk is an added feature. Either way, after a few trial runs to the grocery store, you find what child is compatible with another.

Supply lists must be gone over in great detail. Plan menus ahead for each meal. Once we went on a picnic and stayed four days, we had enough food along, but I did make a trip back to town for extra gear. I take advantage of the fact that there usually isn't a store close at hand to let the children rediscover raw vegetables, fruit, and natural foods.

A few confections are tucked in for energy on the trail or to calm a distraught child. Every morning is a Sunday morning breakfast at camp with hotcakes, eggs, bacon, or ham, and orange juice, lunch is always something hot and a sandwich. Dinner, even at camp can be a gourmet's delight. Nothing compares with steak cooked over the campfire or baked potatoes hot from the coals. We insist on keeping healthy fare on the table if our outing will be longer than an afternoon picnic. All stews, spaghetti, chili, or any one dish meal is cooked on the campfire.

We pack very few cans with the exception of soup. A large insulated ice chest is the handiest container for perishables. Use block ice rather than cubed, it will last longer. Set chest in shade and cover with a blanket or sleeping bag. Use lighter cuts of meat first. If meat has been pre-frozen, refrigeration should last for five days in hot weather. That is if no child hunting for extra rations doesn't leave the lid open.

Well-planned recreation is necessary if you're all to relax. Physical activities usually take care of themselves. We add lawn darts and Frisbees, inner tubes and water toys, and balls for playing catch. Each child's personality must be taken into consideration. Include light-reading material, something that can be re-read without becoming monotonous. Individual small games that can be played alone are needed. Plenty of paper and pencils are preferred over color crayons. Pencils won't melt in the back car window! Many games can be improvised from playing cards and a young child should have his favorite toy along. A radio, battery-powered, keeps you abreast of the news and weather changes.

A family cannot relate as a whole for a full day while camping, any more than it can at home. Father and I have found that everyone is more sociable and relaxed when topics are discussed individually, keeping away from classroom procedure as much as possible. The only group sessions are held around the campfire at night when all are in a responsive mood. Astrology is our main topic at this time and we discuss interesting events of the day.

Our 9x12-umbrella tent sleeps six comfortably, though I'm sure the manufacturer would be surprised. It's held more in an emergency. We end the day with a repertoire of songs after everyone is bedded down for the night, which gives neighbors some very humorous entertainment.

Small suitcases were purchased for each child at the Salvation Army store in which they can keep track of their own things. Don't take unnecessary clothes. Swimming suits that dry easily, short sets that don't require ironing, sweaters for cool hours, blue jeans, and warm jackets in case of foul weather. Tennis shoes are indispensible and we take a good boot and warm socks. I might add that one set of clothes are kept for activities away from camp. Most laundering is done in camp with each child taking his or her turn packing water and hanging clothes. If the water is warm enough, we might wash in the river and dry on the bush. Good ropes should be taken for clotheslines. If a laundromat is handy, use it sparingly or it will become like a washday at home.

Each year, a record is kept which includes three lists, menus, supplies, and clothing. It's revised to add new ideas and to correct past mistakes. After making your lists and it comes time to pack, your first reaction is shock. Don't get battle fatigue at this early point, think of the fun ahead. Encounter with "there must be a way" and proceed along this line. Juggle everything until it fits. It's well if through the winter months you observe all box boys at the neighborhood store.

You can spend time on rearranging closets and dresser drawers for practice. It always gives me a lift to start the camping year with cleaned cupboards. To avoid complete disaster one person should do the packing alone. Be sure your car carrier, if you use one, fits your car. You might end up on the highway with pack scattered down the road, so says the voice of experience.

The feeling of accomplishment can be overwhelming when the last door shuts and you are on your way. If you've done your homework well, and checked ahead to park headquarters, checked the weather, checked and rechecked your lists, you may now sit back and relax. At this point, if you've been a good commander the children will enjoy the chance to relax also. By trial and error, camping becomes more fun each year.

Dressing for Today

Following is a contract I would like to make with the God of my understanding and myself, so I will be spiritually dressed to go into the battle of everyday living one day at a time.

Girdle of Truth:

Who I am? I will affirm that I am a child of God. I have the right to live without fear of uncertainty and in dignity.

Breastplate of Righteousness:

I will try to keep the I. over the E. God's Intelligence over my Emotions. I will let His righteousness guide me. Instead of reacting to people and situations in an emotional way, I will remember that God is in charge and there is power in His will.

Sandals of the Gospel of Peace:

I will live peaceably with my family and fellowman [as much as lieth in me], and I will help others to be at peace with God and their fellowman.

Shield of Faith:

With God's protective guidance, I will intuitively know what to do in any given situation. I will trust his guidance. I will be secure and without fear in the knowledge that God is powerful, caring, and forgiving.

Helmet of Salvation:

I will not let negative thoughts destroy my peace of mind. I will remember doubts, fear, insecurity, projection, expectations, and rights are detrimental to my emotional well-being. I will avoid trashy thinking. When I find my mind astray, I will pull it into line with principles, slogans, tapes, remembered messages from the group, speakers, positive thoughts.

Sword of the Spirit:

I will read and listen. I will have ready the word of God, selected pages from our books, the promises, etc., so I can instantly put them to use to deal with fear, anger, resentment, guilt, and self-pity.

Could I remember this getting up in the morning?

A House or Home?

It was uncared for, apparently unloved, a meaningless derelict beside a country road. Summer's warmth strangled it in weeds, while winter permeated its shell in desolate coldness and mold. As I wandered its lifeless rooms, I imagined I heard the incessant chatter of playful children. You could feel the warmth of love and sharing that had once been here.

The house cried out in its anguish of neglect. I encountered remnants of forgotten life everywhere I turned. The eaves still protected a baby's bassinet. Children's phonograph records that once entertained them with "Old MacDonald's Farm" lay discarded in a corner. A silver bowl turned black with age would once have held holiday treats. A blur of tears shattered my vision of family photos still sitting on a desk in the corner.

The walls echoing their despair suddenly became too suffocating to bear. Escaping to the cool shade of the back porch, I discovered even here I was unprotected from the houses pleading call. Birdhouses probed the sky, a basketball hoop waited for a child's tossed ball, an old clothesline drew its black pencil marks across the backyard.

Walking out past the pump house, I found myself under a canopy of evergreen trees, surrounded by a carpet of tall ferns. Memories of long ago knifed through my heart. With tears filling my eyes, I knew that once again flowers would witness children playing here and loving the land. Their voices would fill the rooms, the smell of cooking would lay gentle on the air, and there would be work and play together.

Silent voices assured me that again, this house would be a home. The house and I needed each other. Overwhelmed with my happy thoughts, I knew God had given me back a home that had been lost.

My Greatest Talent

Drowsily I snuggled, in the warmth of my bed.
Visions of the passing day, dancing in my head.
Guilty thoughts of wasted time, washed o'er my reverie.
The tasks undone, resolutions unresolved.
Again, I'd spent my time.
Storing my house of memory.

The alarm shattered the morning's silence. For the next half hour, I would forget my good intentions of jumping quickly out of bed, to get a head start on this new day. "No wasted time today," I had promised. Each moment must be spent wisely and efficiently. I had read an article on wasting one's time, and how each moment must be put to some good use. Today was the day for me to start a vital schedule on revising my precious time.

A little body, warm and damp from sleep, crept in under my bedclothes. Curling up into a tight bundle in my arms, it's two tiny feet, cold from morning's floor, found their way into the folds of my night gown. With baby's breath warm upon my cheek, soft words fell upon my ears, "Good morning, Mommy, I love you." We played hide and seek under the covers and giggled together, because we had the whole bed to ourselves. She got lost in a mountain of bedspread and I hiked miles through tangled sheets to rescue her. Soon, the bedroom was full of great warriors, getting ready for a council of the tribes. Finally, shooing them all out to get ready for breakfast, I filed away in memory the warm dampness of a tiny body and a few more wasted moments.

Making up for lost time, I hurriedly put lunch's together and fed each child as they passed through the kitchen. As the older ones went out the door, I wiped maple syrup off my cheeks from their goodbye kisses. "Why do I always get kissed goodbye before they brush their teeth?" I wondered. Carrying my blessings to have a good day with them, I mentally made note to pray for their individual needs during the day as each crossed my mind.

My time now must be put to good use. Checking each of the girl's rooms, I found each bed neatly made, clothes hung properly and toys in neat display. My son's made bed surprised me even though he's the oldest at home now. He's usually too busy philosophizing and can't be bothered with menial tasks like cleaning his room.

Quickly, I did my room and the upper bath. I gave a passing swipe to the hallway as I headed for the breakfast dishes, the floors, and the living room. The phone began its morning clatter. Should this be counted as wasted time? I was informed of a good bargain at a neighborhood store, gave encouragement to a young mother, who thought she'd go mad, raising two small sons, received help on a poem I was writing, met an interesting psychic and received so much from each of whom I talked to, how could it be wasting time?

With the immediate things done, I spent an hour playing in the tub with the youngest. I watched her chubby hands, as they fumbled with each button, her ineptness at brushing her hair, and answered all her inquisitive questions, about where the water goes when it disappears down the drain. Looking rosy and smelling like spring flowers, we stood in front of the television set saying the pledge of allegiance with Miss Margaret and the children on Romper Room. This would surely be classified as wasted time if anyone were to see me now. My four-year-old's insistence on my participation in proceeding word games and exercises, dispelled any guiltiness on my part. While Felix the Cat entertained her imagination, I prepared her lunch. I could put in the wash and do some folding while she ate.

We readied ourselves for a quick trip to the grocery store, and I promised to make up for lost time. My intentions were well intended, but the store becomes a fairyland to a four year-old. "Look at all the fish, Mommy, how come they don't wiggle?" "Where are all the chickens that laid their eggs?" "Is this the same kind of milk that cows give?" A quick trip turned into an exploring adventure of farm machines and modern accomplishments. A look at my watch confirmed the fact that I was a miserable failure at saving time.

The afternoon seemed to be spent in a series of half-finished jobs, when the older children started reappearing home from school. Everyone being famished the kitchen is raided by barbarians who know their pilfering will end in KP duty. Time now is running out, for the master will soon appear through the door. Unlike me, a slave to work time, he will expect a hot dinner and the house in order. Somehow, I've managed to remember to put a roast in the oven. One child is called from her club house in the back closet to set the table. Another makes a salad, while still another puts on a vegetable and has my wasting time forced me into child labor?

Without the time to make a proper deduction, I call on my son to peel potatoes. He readily accepts, as he has just begun home economics at school and welcomes the practice. I, as leader of such a mass of activity, should be the busiest. But I am lost in deep observation. My son sits on a small child's folding chair, with his almost six-foot framework, wrapped around the wastebasket; potatoes are piled in a pan beside him on the floor. Great chunks of peel and potato are disappearing into the container between his knobby knees. Almost poking his eye with the paring knife, he brushes the hair out of his eyes and casts an innocent glance at me. "Do these have to be washed?" He asks. "They surely do." I answer and wonder, why I don't explain the proper way to prepare vegetables to him as I would to the girls. Holding my tongue, I relish the hysterical picture before me and put it away in memory as it is.

When Father arrives, work worn and tired, the scolding I give myself isn't spared. He seems pleased though that his dinner is ready, the house appears clean, and his children throw a barrage of interesting events and thoughts his way. All is well and I don't think he noticed the ironing still wasn't done or that the dust webs still hung from the dining room light fixture. With dishes done and homework put away, the last discussion of the probabilities of reincarnation ended. The final plan discussed for repainting a little girls room, prayers of thanksgiving for a bountiful day said, the argument of who is hogging all of the covers settled, the house grows quiet and I think about all my precious "wasted" moments.

I drowsily snuggle, in the warmth of my bed,
Visions of the passing day, dancing in my head.
Guilty thoughts of wasted time washed o'er my reverie,
But with thankful prayer for my greatest talent;
I've stored my house of memory.

The Cranberry Bog

The sun fought feebly to detain summer's retreat a few days longer. The nippy cold on fingertips and nose belied its every effort.

The air filled my nostrils with the intoxicating smell of fallen leaves, lying in nests of red and gold. The sound of boots softly caressing frost dampened moss intermingles with the occasional cry of a startled blue-jay.

Stooping low to evade the clutches of overhanging salmonberry brush, we quietly made our way along a path fashioned by wild deer and elk. The spongy mat of fallen fir and hemlock needles absorbed the sound of our footfalls and we came upon the hidden cranberry bog unnoticed.

Tree laden hills draped the bog in a circle, so closely it created the illusion of twilight. So quietly we stood, we were afraid the beating of our hearts would give warning of our presence to the bull elk, standing majestically in the center of the bog.

For some time he fed contentedly on the wild cranberries. Then catching an unfamiliar scent or sound, he raised his huge rack of antlers and stared at the strange intruders, who had interrupted his mornings feast.

Moving slowly, as not to seemingly invade his privacy, we stooped to pick the small wine-red berries. Sensing we meant him no harm, he returned to his leisurely breakfast.

Our quota of berries picked, we half-circled the bog to retreat in a different direction from whence we had come.

Adjusting our eyes to the bright sunlight again, my companion looked for a rotten log to rest upon. He reached into shirt pocket retrieving a Bull Durham sack, and proceeded to nimbly roll a brown papered cigarette.

No word had passed between us for the past hour and a half. As the smoke curled upward, our glances mutually met over a silent understanding, that any spoken word would be superfluous.

That day, that remembered moment proceeding Thanksgiving made me aware of the real blessings we have to be thankful for; togetherness, beauty, love, understanding and sharing. All had a new meaning which has been revived each year by this poignant memory.

Thank you, Dad.

For Sanity's Sake

Our peers say we must listen with dutiful ear to our children. Of course I agree, but with an abundance of reservation. I doubt that the authors of such advice have raised seven children, been close with ten nephews and nieces, "adopted" many more became a grandparent at thirty-seven, while there was still a three year-old at home or all of his friends who visited had at least five.

Now, it's my observation that a parent must talk to his children. I can hear the psychologist's remonstrations already. But only through excessive talking have I saved myself from being arrested for child abuse, pill consumption, and delayed sanitarium visits. There is of course a certain amount that reaches my ears which automatically triggers my vocal cords. Thus, I've verbally kept one step ahead of disaster.

When my teenage son walks in and announces he's invited to a weekend root beer party and that he's going with a friend, I have already stopped listening and my mouth has gone into action. "It better be root beer, I'll stand for no snitching at your age." It must be chaperoned by responsible parents. I want their phone numbers and addresses with directions on how to get to their home. Are they members of your church group and does that boy you will be riding with have a valid license, insurance and has he ever been stopped for speeding or reckless driving? You must be home by twelve, wear clean clothes, and burn the trash before you go.

*Received by Senator Edward M. Kennedy and cordially answered.

This article was written during the time the Indians were claiming their fishing rights on the Puyallup.

The earth was still. His footsteps fell softly on the damp carpet of moss. Silence seemed to bore into every pore. He shook his head hard from side to side, to clear the numbness away, so he could hear the steady beating of his heart. He could feel the warmth it spread through his body and it made his fingertips tingle.

For a moment, he stopped and stood very still, poised like a deer in alertness. In that moment, his thoughts traveled back in time to his ancestors before him.

The blood that raced through his veins was a part of them. His heart beat for the same reasons, for the same needs and dreams. All he wanted was the beautiful peace; peace that you could feel so deeply, on a morning such as this, and to care for his own. What price would he pay for the natural act of feeding and clothing his own family?

Numbness came again and there was a dull ache at the back of his head. Cold had crept in under his mackinaw, shivering. He wiped the dampness from his forehead.

He began to move again, a quicker more determined step. A needle of hysterical laughter pierced somewhere within his depths, "See the great warrior going to meet his foe, with empty hands and his only weapon is his heart." His heart, which said he was right and just in demanding his independence not to be taken from him.

He'd inherited the right from his father; and from his father on back down the line to the treaty signing; when the white man proclaimed that his people could live in their peaceful wonderland as they had always done, caring for their own.

He could hear the river now. Its turbulent song used to fill him with thanksgiving, for it was full from bank to bank with the great fish that filled his children during winter and supplied their daily needs. Today, the sound was clouded with uncertainty and fear.

Yes, fear. He knew even great men knew fear. He would do what was expected of him. He would not shame his people or himself. Though his hands were empty and they were many, he carried with him a great heart. Justice was on his side. Someday, somewhere it would have to prevail. Maybe not today, but someday for his children.

A blue-jay startled by his presence, gave a noisy scolding and spread its blue beauty winging to a farther tree. The angry roar of an outboard motor tore at the mornings silence and he rounded the bend of the river.

What lay ahead? Failure in his right to be independent? Failure to fish the great fish of the river to feed his family: Physical harm? Jail? Despair?

He was running now. The air was filled with angry shouts, barely audible over the din of the outboard motors. No time now for thoughts of peace or dreams.

He was now like his ancestors, a warrior going into battle against the forked tongue of the paleface.

Bull of the Woods

He's been called rough,
And he's been called tough.
The bull of the woods they say,
They cuss till they choke.
They blow out blue smoke,
Yet I don't see them this way.

He's the man you see who's laughing in his beer there at the end of the bar. He's happy tonight. Death missed him again and he feels real good. Monday he'll face him again and know him a little bit better. He'll spend this weekend planning how to out fox him next week.

No, he doesn't spend much time talking religion or going to church. But at 4:30 a.m. while the rest of you sleep, he's having his first cup of coffee and listening to H. W. Armstrong preach his morning sermon. Bishop Cushman wrote, "I must meet God in the morning, I want Him through the day." He knows someone watches out for him for he jumped fast enough, and far enough before he even knew why and he stood there with the power saw handles still in his hands and he gave thanks. He doesn't have to sit in a pew to know that Gods greatest commandment was to love one another. He practices this every minute every day by watching out for his crew more than himself.

I think his biggest disappointment was getting out only ten loads and his greatest joy wearing all new work clothes including brand new winter long johns, after they have been washed, of course.

He's the always dirty, sometimes ragged guy, walking home at six; who tracks mud in the front door and throws his tin hat in a corner and bellows with authority and humor, "Where's all my kids?" He's the big tough that picks a spotless baby out of her crib with big dirty hands and lets her know that here's dear old dad and it's a pretty good day after all.

He's the guy who can belch blue smoke at a hang up or call his best friend everything in the book, then turn around and say I'll buy you another beer. He works hard for his money, yet he isn't tight because he might not be around tomorrow to enjoy it. And he'll loan it with no strings attached. Maybe the guy had a bad day too, or maybe he's out of work and has a family like himself.

For all of his rough talk and ways, he's got morals miles long. Like expecting his kids to be responsible for themselves and to work for what they want out of life, to respect authority and mind their manners. Takes just a minute to say yes sir instead of yeah or isn't instead of ain't. If you think you're right speak up and say so, but respect another man's way of thinking also. Come to the table with a shirt on, your mom spent a lot of time fixing right for you today. He's the one with all the patience and knows just how the kids feel about things and takes the time to talk it all out. He's the one that sits on the edge of his son's bed telling him the man's way about that big black eye his sons been toting all evening; and he's the one I caught sneaking ice cream and cake up the stairs to the one that got sent away from the table before dessert time.

He's the one that hasn't got a bad word to say against anyone and doesn't like anyone else saying anything bad against anyone either. He's one of the most patriotic people you'll ever meet. He works out there in God's country every day, and his freedom is priceless. He fought for his country and the right to keep it free and clean and decent for his family.

He works hard for his pay in rain, wind, or snow under hazardous conditions; yet wakes in the morning with humor I can't achieve all day in a warm house.

I see him as the cornerstone of our home, the foundation of our marriage and the leader of which I pray my children will follow.

He's been called rough,
He's been called tough.
The bull of the woods they say,
They cuss till they choke.
They blow out blue smoke,
Yet I don't see them this way.

End of the Trail

Wind whispers through the tree tops, the river sings its melody on its way to the sea and the end of the trail seems so familiar. The fir needled path silences my footsteps and I aimlessly wander as I ponder my life with God at my side.

Yet how completely opposite is the equation of my mind today. Rudyard Kipling's poem "If," always a favorite of mine said, "If you can meet with triumph and disaster and treat those two imposters just the same." What was he thinking? Not a thought I could understand nor accept. However, through a twelve step program, I have found my balance. Life no longer casts unpassable boulders on my trail, just rock slides that can be overcome.

This poetry, writings, and songs are meant as a memento for my family. Most of my iniquities have found healing and I continue to work on character defects that create stumbling on a perfect day.

And to the reader, I'd like to say thank you for sharing your time with me. Putting an old adage into play I'd like to say, "Take what you like and leave the rest." May you find peace at the end of your trail.

> "I have fought the good fight, I have finished the course,
> I have kept the faith."
>
> 2 Timothy 4:7

Songs

"He's My One and All"

I will go, where He bids me to go.
I will do, what He bids me to do.
When I'm tired and wearying so,
I'll find rest and I'll find peace for my soul.

In the darkness of night,
And I have lost my way,
There'll be the brightest light,
To guide me on my way.

When misfortune makes me stumble,
I know that I'll not fall.
For He'll be there beside me,
He's my one and all.

He will hear my plea if I cry,
He'll give solace to my lightest sigh.
And if doubts cloud my way,
He'll hear me when I pray.
I'll find rest and I'll find peace for my soul.

In the darkness of night,
And I have lost my way,
There'll be the brightest light,
To guide me on my way.

When misfortune makes me stumble,
I know that I'll not fall,
For He'll be there beside me,
He's my one and all.

"Trust in Jesus"

Just trust in Jesus,
Call on His name.
Just trust in Jesus,
Forever the same.

He's the only answer,
He's your real friend.
Just trust in Jesus,
Your heartache will end.

He's always there beside you,
He's always there to guide you.
So just trust in Jesus,
Call on His name.
Just trust in Jesus forever the same.

"I Don't Know About Tomorrow"

I don't know about tomorrow,
Or what the day will bring.
But today I'll count my blessings,
Praise through my heart will sing.
I'll remember all the little things,
That you have done for me.
Day by day I'll save each thought,
To place on memory's tree.

Each day while remembering,
Reasons why I love you so.
I'll ask my God to watch over you,
As through this life you go.

There may be untold burdens,
And storms beyond our share.
But I'm going to look for a fair tomorrow,
If I can have your loving care.

I don't know about tomorrow,
Or what the day will bring.
But today I'll count my blessings,
Praise through my heart will sing.
I'll remember all the little things,
That you have done for me.
Day by day I'll save each thought,
To place on memory's tree.

"City Woman"

Oh, roll miles, roll,
Pull, ya horses, pull.
Burn, miles, burn,
Goodbye, city woman.

I've left the city lights,
Flickering just behind.
Rolling down the open road,
With a new life in mind.
There must be a place,
Far enough away from you.
And a gentlewoman,
That won't play me for a fool.

Oh, roll miles, roll,
Pull, ya horses, pull.
Burn, miles, burn,
Goodbye, city woman.

I've got to find a good life,
Around the next bend.
I just need a rest stop,
To let my broken heart mend.
I see the tail lights blinking,
Like a signal from above.
Drawing me away from the city,
And the wrong woman's love

Oh, roll miles, roll,
Pull, ya horses, pull.
Burn, miles, burn,
Goodbye, city woman.

"Wake Up, My Angel"

Come on and wake up,
Come on and wake up.
Wake up my angel,
Wake up and don't be so slow.
Wake up my angel,
You got to show me which way to go.

Ain't had nothing but trouble,
Trouble all the day.
You slept right through my trouble,
You got to come and show me the way.

Wake up, my angel,
You're responsible you know.
Wake up, my angel,
You're supposed to be a pro.

Sleeping on the job,
Ain't going to pay your pension.
Meanwhile I'm living in high voltage tension,
Come on and wake up my angel come on.
Wake up my angel,
Wake up my angel.

Marie E. McFadden

"Sit Still"

Sit still on the highest mountain,
Sit still in the valley far below.
Sit still and listen to each heartbeat,
He will always find you;
This I know.

He's there in the wind from heaven,
He's there in the pine scent you smell.
He's there to take you to glory,
He's there to save you from the depths of hell.

Sit still and know He's your savior,
Sit still and know He's the only way.
Sit still in all your confusion,
He will always guide you;
If you take time out to pray.

"Borrowed Time"

I'm living on borrowed time,
But I don't mind.
For my loving shepherd,
Is waiting for me.

I've got faith as high as mountains,
Strong as the raging sea.
I've got gentle arms to hold me,
And the promise of eternity.
There's no reason for me to worry,
Life is just as it ought to be.

I'm living on borrowed time,
With peace of mind.
For my loving shepherd,
Is waiting for me.

Don't shed any tears of sadness,
I'm as happy as I can be.
To know He really loves me,
And that He's waiting there for me.

I'm living on borrowed time,
But I don't mind.
For my loving shepherd,
Is waiting for me.

MARIE E. McFADDEN

"Let There Be Sunshine"

God said, "Let there be sunshine."
"Let there be night and stars in the sky."
He made a world full of beauty,
A world full of grace for you and I.

Let there be sunshine,
Let there be grace,
And let there be love.

When the whole world is set against you,
And there's no one about you to care.
Turn to God for His devotion,
He'll protect and show you where.

Where there is sunshine,
Where there is beauty.
Where there is grace,
And where there is love.

If your whole world is full of trouble,
And there's trouble where ever you turn.
Reach out for your free salvation,
He has been here and He shall return.

He'll return you to sunshine,
Return you to beauty.
Return you to grace,
And return you to love.

"He Healed Me"

He healed me,
Whole and completely;
I give my thanks to Him.

Broken and bent,
His power He sent;
I give my thanks to Him.

Trusting in Him, holding to His hand,
He healed my body, and I understand.
My life is His,
Through all eternity.
I promised Jesus, for He healed me.

I was in despair,
He gave His loving care.
I gave my thanks to Him,
My soul's at rest.
I have been blest,
I give my thanks to Him.

"Tommy"

I'll marry Tommy, if he'll marry me.
When we get married, we'll raise a family.
He'll have his girl, I'll have his boy.
Then we'll have a couple, more just for joy.
Oh, Tommy, Oh, Tommy,
Won't you marry me?

We'll build a cottage down by the sea
There we'll live forever contentedly.
No more trouble, no more strife,
We'll be together just man and wife.
Oh, Tommy, Oh, Tommy,
Won't you marry me?

Down the rocky road of life,
We'll be together the rest of our lives.
I'll be there in my rockin' chair,
You with your cane and your silvery white hair.
Oh, Tommy, Oh, Tommy,
Won't you marry me?

Marie E. McFadden

"Have a Merry Christmas"

Have a merry Christmas,
You and she alone.
Have a merry Christmas,
While I cry here by the phone.
My poor heart is breaking,
Oh, please think of me.
'Cause I'm asking Santa,
To put you on my Christmas tree.

The sun's no longer in the sky,
The stars have ceased to shine.
All I do is pray that,
One day you'll be mine.
All I do is cry and cry,
And tears roll down my cheeks.
I just sit and wonder why,
And this goes on for weeks.

Have a merry Christmas,
You and she alone.
Have a merry Christmas,
While I cry here by the phone.
My poor heart is breaking,
Oh, please think of me.
'Cause I'm asking Santa,
To put you on my Christmas tree.

"Just a Lullaby"

Poor little babe,
Tears drying on your cheek.
I hear you sob and sigh,
Tossing in your sleep.

Father and I are fighting,
And it's breaking your heart.
There's no way to choose,
You don't want us to part.

Why can't grown-ups see,
Where the hurt really lies?
In the soft baby blue,
Of a three year-old's eyes.

Poor little babe,
Full of grief and sorrow.
Rest now little babe,
Rest for tomorrow,
Rest for tomorrow.

"Without a Home"

He had golden stairs to climb when 'ere he chose,
He had millions of dollars and wore fancy store bought clothes.
He lived in a palace just like a king,
But he was a man without a home;
And he was a man all alone.

There was no one to hold him when he was cold,
He could buy any dolly but he had no one of his own.
He could buy anything but he had no dream,
'cause he was a man without a home;
He was a man all alone.

I'd rather run barefoot in these ragged clothes of mine,
Knowing the kind of man I am.
Keeping my peace of mind,
Than having all the money that this old world can hold.
My heart is never ever cold,
Because of you my darling;
I am a man with love and a home.

MARIE E. McFADDEN

"Time Lost"

I just don't have the time for living,
Or doing all the things I'd like to do.
I don't have the time to hold you,
I just don't have the time for loving you.

All of my time is wishing,
I see it all in the bottom of my glass.
I don't have the time to love you,
I just have the time to reminisce.

Once long ago when the world was new,
I had a love other than you,
And my world came all apart,
And it left me with this broken heart.
Now I just don't have the time for loving you.

Once in a while if I'm not dreaming,
I see you through this cloudy haze.
Then I'd like to try and love you,
But I know I can't change my ways.
I just don't have the time for loving you.

"I'll Pretend"

I'll pretend that I don't love you,
I'll pretend that I don't care.
I'll make believe that I don't want you,
And that I don't look for you everywhere.

But raindrops, snowflakes, and sunshine,
Will remind me every day of the year;
That you've gone away and left me,
Whatever the reason, whatever the season,
It'll be just too lonely to bear.

I'll pretend that it isn't autumn,
That leaves aren't turning red and gold.
And I'll pretend that it isn't winter,
That your love for me hasn't grown cold.

But raindrops, snowflakes, and sunshine,
Will remind me every day of the year;
That you've gone away and left me,
Whatever the reason, whatever the season,
It'll be just to lonely to bear.

I'll make believe that it's still summer,
That the skies are always sunny and blue.
And whatever the season may bring me;
I'll pretend I'm not the world's biggest fool.

But raindrops, snowflakes, and sunshine,
Will remind me every day of the year;
That you've gone away and left me,
Whatever the reason, whatever the season,
It'll be just to lonely too bear.

Marie E. McFadden

"Face This Day All Alone"

I don't have to face this day all alone,
Even though my hopes and dreams are gone.
I know that I can make it on my own,
No one can take away my memories with you.

You walked out the door and said we were through,
But I still have forever to keep on loving you.
I don't need someone else to wipe away my tears,
I have my memories, they'll help me make it through the years.

I don't have to face this day all alone,
Even though my hopes and dreams are gone.
I know that I can make it on my own,
No one can take away my memories with you.

I cry myself to sleep at night remembering how it used to be,
And I pretend sometimes you're still loving me.
You'll go out and find someone that you love more,
But I've closed up my heart and put a lock on my front door.

I don't have to face this day all alone,
Even though my hopes and dreams are gone.
I know that I can make it on my own,
No one can take away my memories with you.

"He Doesn't Know"

He doesn't know,
Even when I tell him so.
That he put the stars back in the sky,
Just for me.
No, he doesn't know.
Even when I tell him so,
That he's the one that set me free.

It had been so long,
Since anyone had cared.
I didn't know if I dared
To love him.

But once again I'll live,
For the love he'll give.
No, he just doesn't know
How much he has done.
He doesn't know,
Even when I tell him so.
He put the warmth
Back in the sun.

He doesn't know,
Even when I tell him so.
How could he know,
How much I love him.

Marie E. McFadden

"Skunks"

I'm a sittin' by the hog pen,
Waitin' for the skunks to drop by.
The hogs are awailin' and groanin',
Beggin' an amoanin',
Thinkin' its feeding time.

While I'm a wishin' and dreamin',
Pining to get my sights in line.
I'm a sittin' by the hog pen,
Waitin' for the skunks to drop by.

Now it really ain't a wrong,
For the skunks to eat the hog food.
But the pen is so close to the barn,
I don't want my little chicks that are in there,
To come to any harm.
So I'm sittin' with old betsy,
Thinkin' about the stink I might smell.
I'm sittin' by the hog pen,
Waitin' for the skunks to go to, well,
I'm waitin' for the skunks to drop by.

"The Widow"

My place used to be lying on your shoulder,
Now you turn your back on me,
And its' not because we're older.
I'm a widow of the bottle,
It's getting so I don't care.
You're going to stagger home one night,
And I won't be waiting there.

Drinking whiskey and gambling,
You throw away your money.
The gals all hang around your neck,
And you have to call them honey.

You're out again tonight and I'm waiting all alone,
I know there'll be a fight,
When you come stumbling home.
I'm a widow of the bottle.
It's getting so I don't care,
You're going to stagger home one night,
And I won't be waiting there.

MARIE E. McFADDEN

"The Shepherds Flock"

During the noonday sun,
They came one by one.
Gathering in a meadow of green,
By the rippling mountain stream.
To the shepherd they came,
In their own special time.
And He calmed their fears, wiped away their tears.
And He gave them love,
And He gave them love.

They came there to find,
Peace of heart and mind.
A place where souls are free,
The land of eternity.
To the shepherd they came,
In their own special time.
He promised them peace and sins release,
And He gave them love,
And He gave them love.

Come to the shepherd,
In your own special time.
Feel the tenderness of His hand,
He'll give peace to all.
Who want to understand,
For He has love,
Oh, yes, He has love.

Marie E. McFadden

"Take a Walk"

I'm going to take a walk,
Take a walk, take a walk away.
I'm going to take a walk,
Take a walk, take a walk and pray.

Smog fills the air,
There's people all around.
Noise beats on my ears,
There's litter on the ground.

I'm going to take a walk,
Take a walk, take a walk away.
I'm going to take a walk,
Take a walk, take a walk and pray.
I'm going to take a walk, where fields are rich and green.
I'm going to take a walk, where the air is sweet and clean.

Forty days in the wilderness,
Finding peace for my soul.
Forty days in the wilderness,
Getting rid of all my woes.

I'm going to take a walk,
Take a walk, take a walk away.
I'm going to take a walk,
Take a walk, take a walk and pray.

I'm going to pray for fields that are rich and green,
I'm going to pray for air that's sweet and clean.
I'm going to take a walk,
Take a walk, take a walk away.
I'm going to take a walk,
Take a walk, take a walk and pray.

"Come You Little Children"

Come you, little children,
Gather round my knee.
Gonna tell you about,
Jesus and me.

Gonna tell you how we,
Stuck it through thick and thin.
Gonna tell you how,
I worship Him.

Come you little children,
Gather round my knee,
Gonna tell you about,
The cross and me.

Gonna tell you,
How He died for my sin.
Gonna tell you how,
I worship Him.

This old world is lost and sore,
Gather round my knee.
I'll tell you more,
Satan's always there,
Knockin' on your door.
He won't win,
If you don't let him in.
Send him on his way.
Get on your knees and pray.

Come you little children,
Gather round my knee.

Marie E. McFadden

"No Greater Love"

There is no greater love,
Than God can give.
There is no greater life,
Than God can give.
He went to the cross and died,
That ye might live.
There is no greater love,
Than God can give.

He'll take your hand and lead,
Just follow Him.
He calmed my troubled heart,
And forgave my sin.
He gave His life for you,
That ye might live.
There is no greater love,
Than God can give.

Are You Just Like Me?

When you wake up in the morning,
And the sun is shining bright.
And the Lord has kept you safely,
Through the long and lonely night.
Maybe you remember,
Or are you just like me?
I admit,- I forget,- to thank thee.

He cares for you daily and takes care of all your needs,
He loves and protects you and takes your hand to lead.
Maybe you remember,
Or are you just like me?
I admit,—I forget,—to thank thee.

Give your heart to Jesus,
And follow all His way.
Don't forget to thank Him,
Every single day.
Now, maybe you'll remember,
Or are you just like me?
I admit,—I forget,—to thank thee.

Marie E. McFadden

"Your Nail Scarred Hand"

Put your nail scarred hand on my shoulder,
And guide me through this night.
Put your nail scarred hand on my shoulder,
And show me your glory bright.

I wondered this land alone,
Not knowing which way to go.
If you're there,
Walking beside me,
I know I'll find peace,
For my soul.

"Try and Convince Me"

Hello there, stranger,
Meet Mrs. Lonely.
Do you mind if I sit next to you?
Please don't think that I'm chasing.
I just need someone I can talk to.
No, you don't have to hold me,
Or wipe tears from my eyes.
Just try and convince me,
Life will get better.
That the sun will shine,
And there'll be bluer skies.

Soon I'll get the papers,
That end my married life.
Then I'll be just Mrs. Lonely,
Instead of some ones wife.
He said that he loved me,
But he had to chase around.
Now I'm all alone,
Even when I'm in a crowd.

Hello there, stranger,
Meet Mrs. Lonely.
Can you tell me what I should do?
With a life full of memories,
That always make me feel blue.
No, you don't have to give me,
Stolen moments to remember.
Just try and convince me,
My heart will stop aching.
And I'll find a new love,
That's warm and tender.

Hello there, stranger,
Meet Mrs. Lonely.

Marie E. McFadden

"Christmas Lullaby"

Hush-a-bye little child,
Don't you cry.
Can't you see there's a new star in the sky?

Wise men on a faraway hill roam,
Following the bright light leading them home.

Hush-a-bye little child,
Close your eyes.
Close your eyes, go to sleep, don't you cry.
Close your eyes,
Go to sleep.
Don't you cry,
For tomorrow will be a new day.

"Give Some Love"

Share His word,
Share His love,
Give a little to the neighbor next to you.

Share your faith,
Share your grace,
Give a little to the neighbor next to you.

Turn around and shake his hand,
Take apart in what Jesus planned.
Give a lot of love,
To the neighbor next to you.
Give him some love,
And he'll give it back to you.

Marie E. McFadden

"The Dust of Material Bondage"

Bring me a handful of pebbles,
Or a few drops of morning's dew.
Hand me a ray of sunshine,
Let me touch a patch of summer's sky blue.
Don't waste my time,
Dreaming of golden mansions.
Don't promise me priceless jewels,
They're only the dust of material bondage;
That blows away in the hands of fools.

If you have but two arms to hold me,
When I'm weary at the end of the day.
Or when I become angry and impatient,
A few tender words you could say.
Lend me a bit of your humor,
When no smile I find of my own.
Promise me a better tomorrow,
Stand by me so I don't stand alone.

Pick me a bouquet of wild flowers,
Buy me a rooster that crows at dawn.
Share with me but one quiet moment,
To build my dreams upon.
Don't waste my time,
Dreaming of golden mansions.
Don't promise me priceless jewels,
They're only the dust of material bondage;
That blows away in the hands of fools.

"Afterglow"

All that is mine,
Is the afterglow.
The afterglow,
Of a raging fire.
And to my solitude,
I retire,
With the afterglow
Of your burning lips,
On mine.

I know that you are gone,
That I will always be alone.
But I'll hold close to my heart,
The afterglow
Of a love,
That was my own.

Marie E. McFadden

"Until You Walk Back Through the Door"

I watched you finish breakfast,
With soft and sleepy eyes.
The sun was just arising,
In dawns chilly winter skies.
I hate to see you go out,
In the early mornings cold.
I'd like to keep you home with me,
To love and to hold.
But my day just won't begin,
Until you walk back through the door.

I'll gently kiss each cherub face,
And send them on their way.
I'll say a prayer for each of you,
While you're gone from me today.
I'll do all the little things,
I know will please you more.
But my day just won't begin,
Until you walk back through the door.

I'll go into make the bed,
And I'll see where your tossed head
Lay close to mine last night.
I'll remember your gentle kiss.
The warmth of tender loving bliss,
When your arms held me tight.
I'll spend the day thinking of you,
While I tend to every chore,
But my day just won't begin;
Until you walk back through the door.

I'll pick up the spare tire,
Bake the cake for PTA.
I'll pay the monthly bills,
Ones you forgot to pay.
I'll hang up your clothes,
Polish your shoes.
Do the shopping at the store,
But my day just won't begin.
Until you walk back through the door.

MARIE E. McFADDEN

Printed in the United States
By Bookmasters